ERIC and LUCY KINCAID'S

TALES of MAGIC and ENCHANTMENT

BRIMAX BOOKS

Cambridge · England

CONTENTS

NILS IN THE FOREST
(A Danish story)

Nils had spent the morning gathering firewood in the forest. When his sack was full with dry twigs he sat down under a tree, and took out his dinner. He had just unwrapped his bread and was about to take a bite from his cheese when a tiny dwarf with a long yellow beard appeared from nowhere and stood in front of him.

"Spare a coin so that a hungry old man can buy food," said the dwarf, holding out his wrinkled hand.

"I'm sorry," said Nils, "I have no coins, but I will gladly share my bread and cheese with you." And without waiting for the dwarf to reply he gave him half of what he had.

The dwarf ate hungrily and didn't leave a crumb. When he had finished Nils handed him his flask. "Wash it down with some ale," he said.

The dwarf drank exactly half, no more and no less, and handed the flask back to Nils. Then, without warning, he clapped his hands and disappeared as suddenly as he had appeared.

"Well I never," said Nils, when he had got over his surprise. "And not even a thank you for eating half my dinner."

Nils was on his way home, with the sack of firewood over his shoulder, when the trees around him began to tremble, and the ground beneath his feet began to shake.

'What can be happening?' thought Nils, trembling more than a little himself. He wasn't long finding out. Suddenly, towering high above the trees, was a troll wife. Some trolls are small. Some are big. Some are very big. And some are VERY BIG INDEED. This troll wife was even bigger than that. She was simply ENORMOUS!

"What are you doing in MY forest?" she roared, in a voice as loud as thunder.

"G.g.gathering firewood . . ." shivered Nils.

"No one gathers firewood in MY forest!" roared the troll wife. "I shall eat YOU for my supper."

"Please . . . don't do that. I have a wife and seven children at home. How will they live without me to look after them?"

The troll wife was in a playful mood. "Run and hide," she said, "and I will come and look for you. The first time I find you I will let you go. The second time I find you I will also let you go. But the third time I find you I shall EAT YOU . . . now off with you . . . run and hide!"

Nils dashed here, there, and everywhere in a panic. How could he hide from a troll wife? It was impossible. He had almost given up hope of escaping alive when the dwarf with the long yellow beard re-appeared.

"Do not worry," said the dwarf. "I will hide you." And taking his axe he chopped a splinter from a tree trunk. "In you go," he said. He pushed Nils into the space left by the splinter, then put the splinter back on top of him.

"She will never find you in there," laughed the dwarf.

10

He laughed too soon. When the troll wife came looking for Nils she was carrying an axe.

"Where are you going?" asked the dwarf.

"To cut down a tree, of course," said the troll wife. And she cut down the very tree in which Nils was hiding.

"Found you!" she said as she pulled him out. "Run and hide again," she said as she put him on the ground.

"Come with me," whispered the dwarf. He led Nils out of the forest and to the side of a lake where there were thick reed beds. He tapped Nils on the shoulder and Nils shrank to the size of a pin. Then the dwarf took a reed, broke it in two, put Nils inside the hollow stem, put the two halves of reed together, and put the reed back into the reed bed.

"She will NEVER find you in there," laughed the dwarf.

"Where are you going?" he asked, as the troll wife came up behind him with a sharp knife.

"Where do you think? To cut reeds of course." And with one big swish, she had cut them all.

11

"Found you!" she laughed, as she shook the reeds and Nils tumbled to the ground. "Now run and hide once more. Next time I find you I shall put you in my cooking pot."

Nils was in despair.

"Worry not," said the dwarf. "We'll outwit her yet." He dipped his hand into the lake and caught a fish. He broke it in two and placed Nils inside it. Then he joined the two halves together and threw the fish back into the lake. It swam away with a quick wiggle of its tail, and with Nils safe inside.

When the troll wife came looking for Nils she was carrying a wash tub and a fishing net.

"Where are you going?" asked the dwarf.

"To catch a fish for my supper of course," she laughed.

She pushed the wash tub into the water and climbed into it herself. She paddled with her hands until she was in the middle of the lake, then she took her fishing net and dipped it into the smooth, calm water.

"I can see the VERY fish I am looking for," she called.

The dwarf, who was watching from the shore, bent close to the waters edge and began to blow. He blew and he blew and he BLEW. What a storm he blew up. The wind howled! The thunder roared! The smooth lake became a raging sea. The waves grew higher, and rougher and rougher. The wash tub pitched, and turned and tumbled.

"Mercy! Mercy!" screamed the troll wife, clinging desperately to the sides of the wash tub.

"If you have ever shown mercy, then mercy will be shown to you," said the dwarf. Instantly, the wash tub overturned and tipped the troll wife into the lake. She was so heavy she sank straight to the bottom and was never seen again.

As soon as the dwarf was sure she was gone for good he stopped blowing and the lake became as calm as a puddle. He caught the fish, broke it open, took Nils out and restored him to his proper size. Then he put the fish together again and threw it into the lake. It swam away with a merry swish of its tail and without a backward glance.

The dwarf took Nils to the cave where the troll wife had lived. It was full of gold.

"Take it," said the dwarf. "It is all yours."

"Thank you . . . " gasped Nils.

"And thank you for the dinner you so kindly shared with me," said the dwarf. And with that he clapped his hands and vanished.

Nils never saw the dwarf again, but there was never a day which passed when he did not think of him, and the strange adventures that followed his appearance.

THE MAGIC BOOK

James Julian Smith worked for a wizard. Not mixing spells
of course, the wizard did that himself, but dusting test tubes
and apparatus, sweeping the floor, sticking labels onto jars of
frogs legs, sorting ladybird eggs, and looking after all the
other mysterious and wonderful things that wizards use. His
most important job was dusting the magic book in which the wizard
wrote all his spells.

The book was bound in leather
and was so important it was chained
to a table, and the table itself
was fixed to the floor. It was
very thick, and smelled of long
ago, and mystery. It was a smell
to make any nose tingle with
excitement. James Julian wanted
to see inside the magic book more
than anything else in the world.
The wizard used it every day, but
whenever James Julian tried to
look over his shoulder the wizard
would bang the book shut and wait
for him to go away. Whenever he
had finished working on a spell
he would lock the clasp of the
book and put the key in his
pocket.

15

One day, the wizard went out on a collecting errand. There was a special ingredient he wanted for a spell and only he knew where it could be found.

"Carry on dusting," said the wizard, popping his favourite frog into his pocket as he went out.

"Yes Your Wizardship!" said James Julian.

He decided to start by dusting the book. Flick went the duster, flick . . . flick . . . James Julian stroked the leather cover gently with his finger . . . and made a startling discovery.

The book was unlocked! The wizard had FORGOTTEN TO LOCK THE BOOK!

James Julian stood staring at the book for a whole minute before he dared to open it. He turned the pages very carefully. Each one was covered with spidery writing and strange marks and symbols. James Julian couldn't understand ANY of it.

If only HE could cast a spell. Just ONE spell. Just a LITTLE one. He moved his finger along one of the lines of writing and began to read strange words that sounded like gobbledy gook. There was a swishshshsh! A rush of cold air! A swirl of hissing round his ears! James Julian slammed the book shut so fast he almost caught his nose in it. He wasn't fast enough. The magic words he had just read had summoned a demon.

"What task do you set me?" asked the demon, hissing like a volcano.

James Julian was trembling so much he couldn't think of anything to say at all.

"Set me a task or I will strangle you," said the demon as though it was something he did every day.

"W.w.w.water that!" gasped James Julian pointing to a flower-pot standing beside the desk.

"It shall be done!" said the demon and left the room. He returned carrying a large barrel full to the very brim with water.

"No . . NO . . . NOT THAT MUCH!" gasped James Julian, "YOU'LL MAKE EVERYTHING ELSE WET!"

But it would seem that the demon had suddenly gone deaf for he poured every drop of water in the barrel over the flower growing in the flowerpot. James Julian was right. It WAS too much. It DID make everything else wet. It washed the flower right out of the flowerpot.

But the demon had not
finished. He fetched another
barrel of water and emptied that
over the flowerpot too . . . and then
another . . . and another . . . and then
another. And all the time the
demon was pouring, James Julian
was shouting "STOP! STOP! Oh
please STOP!" His voice got
very hoarse.

Before long the water was
swishing round James Julian's
knees.

Soon it reached his waist.
Pieces of apparatus began to
bob about like ducks on a pond.

"The book! I must save the
book!" James Julian grabbed the
precious book from the desk and
held it as high above his head
as the chain would let him.
Still the demon kept filling,
and emptying, the barrel. The
water crept higher and higher.

"Go away . . . oh, please go
away . . . " James Julian's voice
was worn to a whisper.

The water was already lapping round his chin. Any more
and it would be over his head. James Julian couldn't hold his
breath for ever. What WAS going to happen to him?

But just when he thought he was going to drown, the wizard
returned home. The wizard knew EXACTLY the right words to dismiss
the demon, send the water rushing out of the door, and the
apparatus whizzing back to the shelves.

"At least you managed to keep the book dry," said the
wizard as he took the book from James Julian's upstretched arms,
"and it looks as though your arms will ache for a week, so we'll
say no more, but let this be a lesson to you. Do not meddle
with things you do not understand."

"Oh, I'll never do it again," said James Julian. And he
didn't, but that was because the wizard never left the magic book
unlocked again, and he didn't get the chance.

POET, GOBLIN AND DONKEY

Once there was a poet who could make up songs that would entice the fish from the sea, the birds from the sky, and the worms from the ground. The words he sang were as magical as any spell.

One day, the Queen's daughter fell into a sulk. The Queen sent for the poet.

"Your Majesty," he said, bowing very low. "Can I be of service?"

"The Princess woke this morning with a pimple on the end of her nose," said the Queen. "The only thing I know of that will cure it is the magic . . . "

"Oh, how kind," interrupted the poet. "How kind to say the magic of my songs will charm away a pimple and restore the Princess to her former beauty . . . "

"Don't interrupt . . . " said the Queen. "That wasn't what I was going to say at all. The only thing that will cure it in time for the ball tonight, is the magic ointment owned by the Goblin of the Rock. I command you to go and get it."

"But the goblin hasn't been seen for at least a hundred years," said the poet. "He NEVER leaves the rock."

"Then try your magic songs on him . . . " said the Queen.

It was a royal command, so the poet had to go.

The goblin was curled into a
tight ball in the very heart of
the rock. He was deaf to the
world, or so everyone thought.

The poet knew it was going
to be difficult. He knew he
would have to sing as he had
never sung before. He sang
softly with strange mysterious
words, and at last there was a
faint stirring inside the rock.
Presently the top of the goblin's
bald little head began to show.
The poet could see his forehead
. . . then two slanting eyes . . . then
a long pointed nose . . . then thin
lips . . . and a round chin. Then
two knobbly shoulders appeared.

The poet was drawing the goblin from the rock as gently and
as surely as a maiden draws a fine thread from a bundle of flax.
Now the tops of the goblin's spindly arms were showing . . . now his
bony elbows . . . now the poet could see the hand holding the precious
bowl of ointment . . .

At that precise moment a donkey brayed, right beside the poet's elbow. "EEE! AAWWW!" The poet's song had charmed HIM out of his stable, across a field, over a stream, through a wood, over a hill . . .

"EEE! AWW!" he brayed again, as though to say, "I've come!"

The poet was startled out of his wits and fell over backwards. The goblin was so frightened he shot high into the air in a tangle of arms and legs and rock dust.

Before the poet could recover his senses enough to catch him the goblin had disappeared into a new hiding place carrying the precious ointment with him.

And that's how it was that a proud princess went to a ball hiding the pimple on the end of her nose behind a fan.

It all goes to show that a poet's spell can be broken as easily as any other spell and that sometimes a poet can be too clever by half.

THE GIANT AND THE COBBLER

Once there was a grumpy giant who didn't like anyone very much. But more than anyone else he disliked the people who lived in the town of Shrewsbury. One day, he made up his mind he would get rid of them all – ALL the men, ALL the women, ALL the children and ALL the babies.

Running close by the town of Shrewsbury there was a river.

"I'll dam the river," said the giant, "and flood the town. Then everyone who lives there will drown."

It is very easy indeed for someone as big as a giant to dam a river. All he has to do is lift a spade full of earth – a giant spade of course – and drop the earth in the right place.

The giant was really rather stupid. Instead of waiting till he got to Shrewsbury before filling his spade with earth, which he could have done quite easily, he filled it with earth outside his own cave.

It was a hot day. And even giants get tired, especially when they are carrying a lot of crumbly earth they are trying hard not to spill. Somewhere, it must have been when he stubbed his toe on a boulder and almost dropped the earth on his own foot, he missed the way.

"I appear to be lost," he said, and sat down beside the road – still holding the spade of earth – and waited for someone to come and tell him which direction to take.

Presently, a cobbler, who had been to Shrewsbury himself to collect all the boots and shoes that needed mending, came by.

"Hallo there!" boomed a voice high above the cobbler's head. The cobbler thought at first a hill had spoken. "How far is it to Shrewsbury?"

The cobbler was surprised, but he wasn't one to frighten easily and he thought to himself, 'Ho, ho, what can a giant like THAT be doing with a spade full of earth like THAT . . . he's up to no good, I'll be bound.' Aloud he said, "Why do you want to know?"

"I'm going to dam the river and flood the town so that all the people who live there will drown," said the giant.

'Something must be done about this . . . and quickly,' thought the cobbler.

"Do you know how far it is to Shrewsbury?" he asked.

"I do not," said the giant, and because he was lazy as well as stupid, he added, "Not very far I hope."

"I've just come from there myself," said the cobbler, who was as quick-witted as the giant was stupid. "It's been a very tiring journey I must say." He opened his sack and tipped all the worn boots and shoes he had collected for mending onto the ground. "That's how many boots and shoes I've worn out since I left Shrewsbury," he said.

"Really?" said the giant, looking surprised.

"Yes, really," said the cobbler, his fingers crossed behind his back because he wasn't telling the truth.

"Then it must be a very long way indeed," said the giant.

"Oh, it is," said the cobbler with a tired sigh, although the town of Shrewsbury was just over the next hill and if the giant had listened carefully he could have heard the town hall clock striking the hour.

25

"I can't possibly carry a spadeful of earth THAT far," complained the giant.

"If I were you I'd leave it here and go home," said the cobbler putting the boots and shoes back into his sack.

"That's good advice," said the giant, and tipped the earth off his spade. It fell with a roar, like a cloud burst of dark brown rain, and when the brown dust had cleared the cobbler was standing beside a new hill. The giant was scraping his boots with the spade. There was enough earth sticking to them to make a small hill beside the big one.

The giant went home and I'm glad to say forgot about the people of Shrewsbury. The cobbler mended all the worn boots and shoes and returned them to their rightful owners.

The two hills the giant made are there to this day. And so is the town of Shrewsbury, thanks to the quick thinking of a quick-witted cobbler.

A POT OF GOLD

Patrick lived with his mother, and a cow and some hens, in a tiny cottage in the middle of Ireland. They were poor, but they were happy.

Every morning, as she blew on the peat fire to make it hot enough to cook their breakfast porridge, Patrick's mother would call, "Wake up, and get up, you lazy boy! You will never catch a leprechaun with your eyes closed."

Leprechauns are fairy shoemakers. They live in holes in the ground and between the roots of trees. They are said to be very rich, and wherever there is a leprechaun there is sure to be a pot of gold hidden somewhere close by.

There were leprechauns living near the cottage where Patrick lived with his mother. The wind had only to stop blowing for an instant and Patrick's keen ears could hear the sound of their tiny hammers hammering against leather.

It was Patrick's dearest
wish to find a pot of gold.
But first he had to find a
leprechaun to show him where
there was one hidden.

"If you happen to see a
leprechaun," said Patrick's
mother, at least once every
day, "Do not take your eyes
off him for a moment. If you do
he will disappear and then you
will never find a pot of gold."

One day, when Patrick was
returning home after another
fruitless search, he heard the
sound of tapping. He looked
down, and there, in the long
grass at his feet, was a
leprechaun. He was so busy,
hammering away at a pair of
hob-nailed boots, he hadn't
noticed Patrick.

Patrick moved very quickly.

"Got you!" he cried as he caught the leprechaun in his hand.

"Let me go! Let me go!" shouted the leprechaun, struggling to get free.

"Tell me where your gold is hidden first!"

"G.g.gold . . . " The leprechaun turned very pale.

"Yes . . . tell me . . . or I will not let you go . . . not EVER!"

"Quick! Look behind you! There's a cow in the corn!" cried the leprechaun.

Just in time, Patrick remembered NOT to look.

"Ha . . . ha . . . you don't catch me that way. I won't take my eyes off you. Now where is your pot of gold?"

"I haven't got a pot of gold . . . " cried the leprechaun. "Quick! Look behind you! Your house is burning!"

Patrick almost did look THAT time.

"You're holding me too tight," squealed the leprechaun. "You're squeezing the breath out of me!"

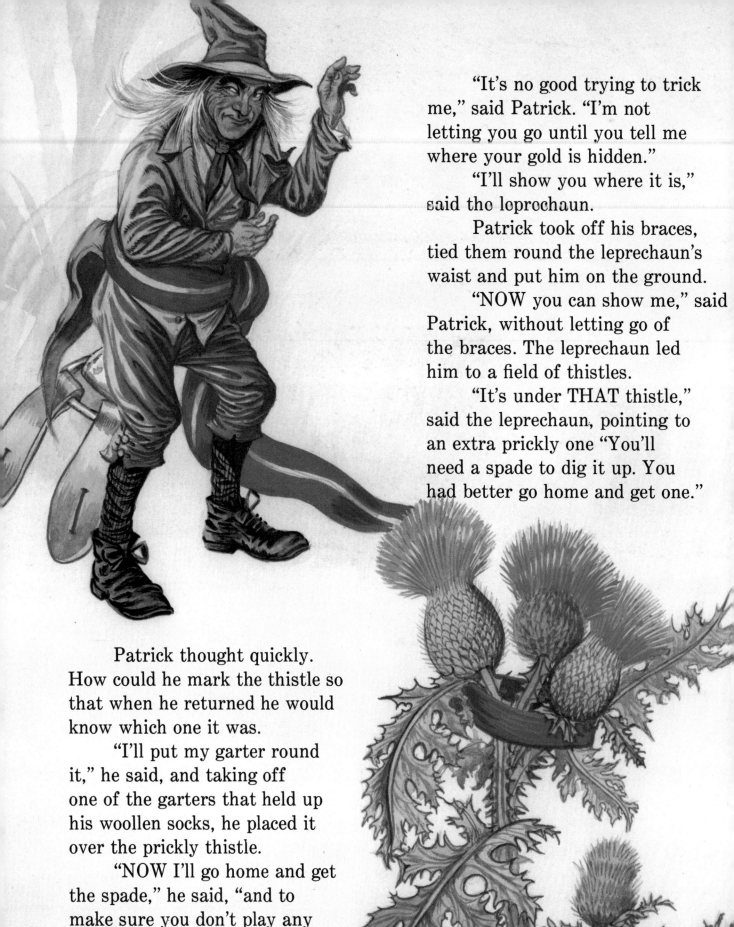

"It's no good trying to trick me," said Patrick. "I'm not letting you go until you tell me where your gold is hidden."

"I'll show you where it is," said the leprechaun.

Patrick took off his braces, tied them round the leprechaun's waist and put him on the ground.

"NOW you can show me," said Patrick, without letting go of the braces. The leprechaun led him to a field of thistles.

"It's under THAT thistle," said the leprechaun, pointing to an extra prickly one "You'll need a spade to dig it up. You had better go home and get one."

Patrick thought quickly. How could he mark the thistle so that when he returned he would know which one it was.

"I'll put my garter round it," he said, and taking off one of the garters that held up his woollen socks, he placed it over the prickly thistle.

"NOW I'll go home and get the spade," he said, "and to make sure you don't play any tricks on me I'll put you in my pocket."

30

Patrick ran home, got a spade and ran all the way back. But when he reached the field, instead of digging, he sat down and howled. He cried and he sobbed. He held his head in his hands. Tears as big as raindrops rolled down his cheeks. Someone – I wonder who – had put a scarlet garter round every thistle in that field. There wasn't ONE thistle that did not have a scarlet garter for a belt. The leprechaun had tricked him after all. His mother had told him not to take his eyes off the leprechaun, hadn't she, and when Patrick put the leprechaun in his pocket that is exactly what he had done. He never saw another leprechaun and so he never found a pot of gold. His mother said, it was entirely his own fault.

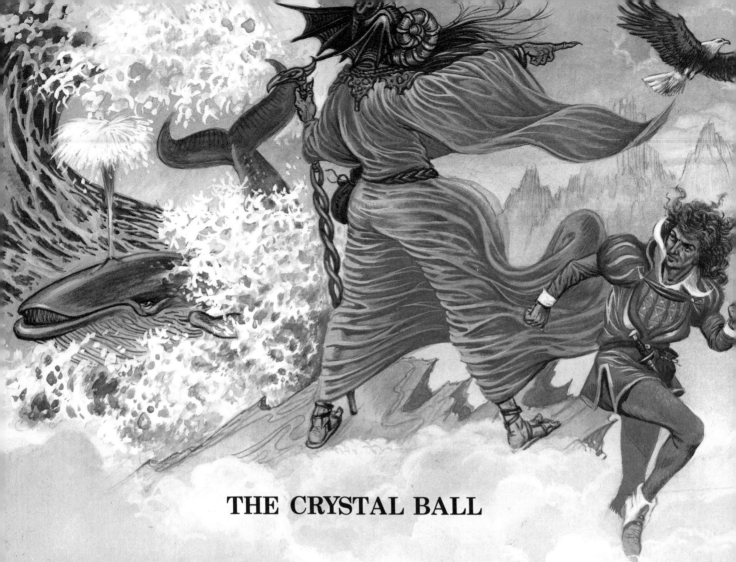

THE CRYSTAL BALL

Once there was an enchantress who had three sons. She did not trust them for she was afraid they would steal her magic powers if they had the chance. She changed the eldest into an eagle and sent him to live in the rocky mountains. His brothers often saw him soaring amongst the clouds. She changed the second into a whale. He was condemned to live in the sea.

When Richard, the youngest of her sons, saw what she had done to his brothers he ran away before she could cast a spell on him.

He had many adventures, and then one day he heard about a king's daughter who was imprisoned in the Castle of the Golden Sun. Several brave men had tried to rescue her but they had all perished. Richard was brave, even though he had run away from his mother's magic, and he decided he would try to rescue the princess himself.

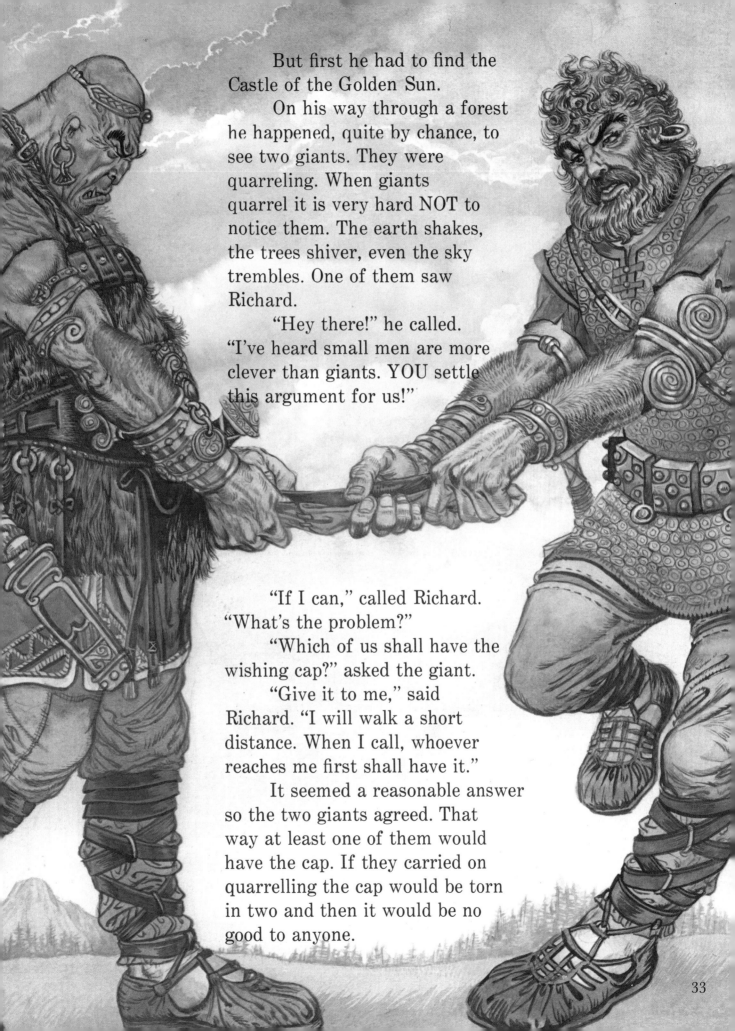

But first he had to find the Castle of the Golden Sun.

On his way through a forest he happened, quite by chance, to see two giants. They were quarreling. When giants quarrel it is very hard NOT to notice them. The earth shakes, the trees shiver, even the sky trembles. One of them saw Richard.

"Hey there!" he called. "I've heard small men are more clever than giants. YOU settle this argument for us!"

"If I can," called Richard. "What's the problem?"

"Which of us shall have the wishing cap?" asked the giant.

"Give it to me," said Richard. "I will walk a short distance. When I call, whoever reaches me first shall have it."

It seemed a reasonable answer so the two giants agreed. That way at least one of them would have the cap. If they carried on quarrelling the cap would be torn in two and then it would be no good to anyone.

Richard put the cap on his own head and began to walk, but he was so busy thinking his own thoughts he forgot to call out to the giants. "Ah," he sighed, "if only I could find the Castle of the Golden Sun." No sooner had he spoken than he was standing outside the castle gates. The wishing cap really was a proper wishing cap.

Richard found the king's daughter in a room deep in the heart of the castle. He couldn't help gasping when he saw her. She was SO wrinkled, and SO ugly, he wanted to turn his head away.

"This is not my real form," said the princess. "I have been bewitched. You may see how I really appear in the mirror, for a mirror cannot lie." The princess looked into her hand mirror so that Richard could see her reflection. She was very beautiful.

"How can the spell be broken?" asked Richard.

"He who holds the crystal ball in front of the Enchanter will destroy his power and I will become myself again," said the princess.

"Where can I find the crystal ball?" asked Richard.

"You must kill the wild bull that lives at the foot of the mountain. From it will spring a fiery bird which has in its body a red hot egg. The crystal ball lies in the yolk of the egg. You must make the bird drop the egg, but if it falls to the ground it will burn everything near it, and the egg and the crystal ball will melt. If that happens then the spell will never be broken." A tear fell onto her cheek.

"Do not cry," said Richard.

He found the bull exactly where the princess said he would. He killed the bull as the princess said he must and from its body rose the fiery bird. It rose into the sky and was about to disappear into the mountains when an eagle appeared. It was Richard's own brother in his enchanted form. As Richard watched, the eagle chased the fiery bird towards the sea. They were almost at the waters edge when the fiery bird dropped the egg.

It fell onto the roof of a fisherman's hut standing on the shore. Flames leapt from the thatch. Smoke billowed into the sky. Soon the egg, and the crystal ball it carried, would be melted in the heat

Just as Richard thought all was lost, a whale, Richard's second enchanted brother, swam close to the shore and caused a great wave to swell up over the beach. The rush of water swept right over the hut and put out the fire.

Richard searched in the wet
ashes until he found the egg.
The cold sea water had cooled it
so quickly the shell had cracked.
Richard peeled away the broken
pieces and found the crystal
ball inside, quite unharmed.

The Enchanter shuddered when he saw Richard had the crystal
ball.

"My power has gone," he said. "YOU are now the King of
the Castle of the Golden Sun." Then he left the castle never to
return.

Richard married the king's daughter and with the crystal
ball restored his two brothers to their rightful shape. They
all lived happily ever after, in the Castle of the Golden Sun.

MOLLY WHUPPIE

Once there was a poor woodcutter who found it impossible to feed all his children. One day he took the three youngest to the forest and left them there.

The children wandered, lost and hungry, until they came to a house. Molly Whuppie, who was the youngest, but by far the cleverest, knocked at the door.

"Please, will you give us something to eat?" she asked.

"Don't you know my husband is a giant and will eat YOU if he gets a chance?" said the woman who had opened the door.

"Please . . ." begged Molly Whuppie. "We are so hungry."

"Very well," said the giant's wife, and took them inside and gave them bread and milk.

When the giant came home for his supper he looked at the three strange children sitting at the table, and said, "Who are they?"

"Just three little children, very poor and thin," said his wife. "You eat your supper, I will look after them."

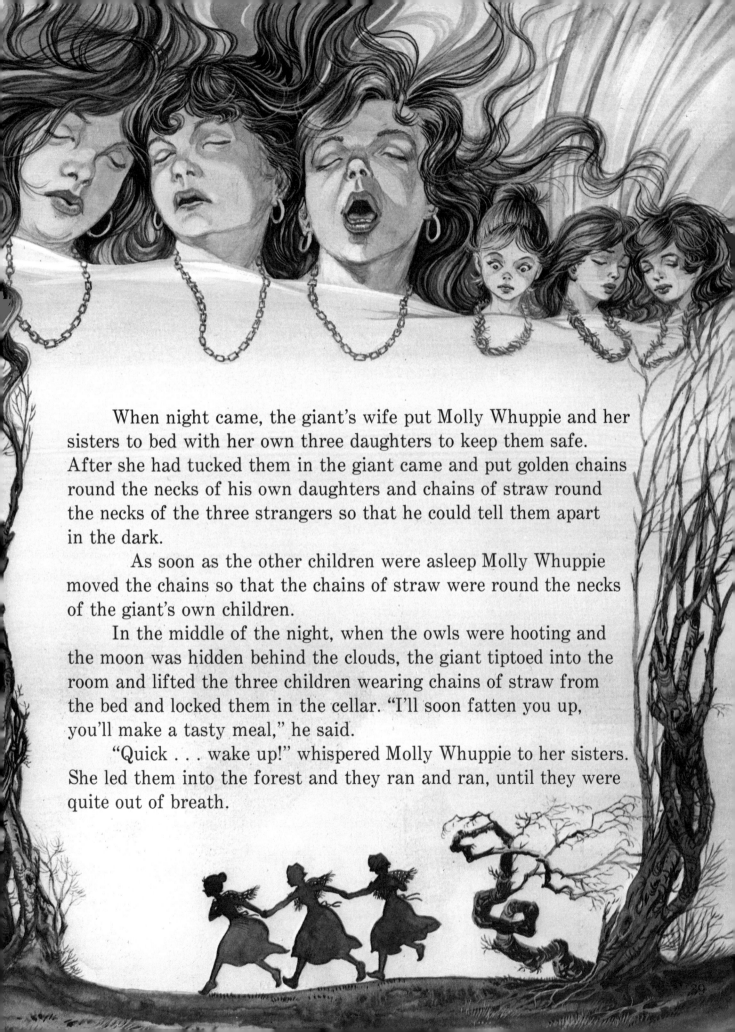

When night came, the giant's wife put Molly Whuppie and her
sisters to bed with her own three daughters to keep them safe.
After she had tucked them in the giant came and put golden chains
round the necks of his own daughters and chains of straw round
the necks of the three strangers so that he could tell them apart
in the dark.

As soon as the other children were asleep Molly Whuppie
moved the chains so that the chains of straw were round the necks
of the giant's own children.

In the middle of the night, when the owls were hooting and
the moon was hidden behind the clouds, the giant tiptoed into the
room and lifted the three children wearing chains of straw from
the bed and locked them in the cellar. "I'll soon fatten you up,
you'll make a tasty meal," he said.

"Quick . . . wake up!" whispered Molly Whuppie to her sisters.
She led them into the forest and they ran and ran, until they were
quite out of breath.

Next day they came to a house that stood beside a lake, and was surrounded by statues, and beautiful gardens. It was the house of a King. He invited them in and Molly Whuppie told him how they had tricked the giant.

"Ho, ho," laughed the King. "Well done! But I know of a better trick. If you go back to the giant's house and bring me the small sword which hangs beside his bed, your eldest sister shall marry my eldest son."

Molly Whuppie had to agree, that if she could do it, that would be a very good trick indeed. That night she went back to the giant's house and hid under his bed.

When the giant was snoring loud enough to make the rafters ring, Molly Whuppie took down the sword and crept towards the door. She was almost there when the sword rattled in its scabbard.

The giant woke with a roar!
"Steal my sword, would you!"
he shouted. He jumped from the
bed with a thud that shook the
whole house and ran after Molly
Whuppie. Molly was very nimble
and very quick, she dodged in and
out of the trees until they came
to the Bridge of One Hair. And
there the giant stopped chasing
her. The Bridge of One Hair,
crossed a very deep ravine. If
the giant had put one foot on it,
the bridge would have broken and
he would have been dashed to
pieces on the rocks below.
Molly Whuppie, who was as light
as a feather, skipped over the
bridge and escaped.

When her eldest sister had been married to the King's eldest son, the King said,

"That was a good trick you played on the giant, but I know of one better. Bring me the purse which lies under the giant's pillow and your second sister shall marry my second son."

That night, Molly Whuppie hid under the giant's bed again. When the giant was snoring fit to shake the roof from the house, she slipped her hand under his pillow and pulled out the purse. She had just reached the door when a coin dropped from the purse and rolled across the floor.

The giant woke with a roar! "Steal my purse, would you!" he shouted. He jumped from the bed with a thud that shook the house so hard a brick fell from the chimney. He chased after Molly Whuppie but she reached the Bridge of One Hair before he did and skipped over it to safety.

When Molly Whuppie's second sister had married the King's second son, the King said,

"That was a good trick you played, Molly Whuppie, but I know of one better. If you bring me the ring which the giant wears on his finger YOU shall marry my youngest son." Molly Whuppie thought THAT was a very good idea indeed, so that night she went back to the giant's house for the third time.

When the giant was snoring fit to shake down a whole forest, she slipped the ring from his finger. She was just putting it into her pocket when the giant opened one eye, very, very slowly, and looked at her.

"Steal my ring would you!" he whispered, though HIS whisper was as loud as a gale, and he caught hold of her.

"Let me go . . . let me go . . ." shouted Molly Whuppie.

The giant looked at her and said, "What would YOU do to ME, if I had tricked YOU as YOU have tricked ME?"

"I would put you in a sack with a dog and a cat, and a needle and a thread, and a pair of scissors. I would hang you up against the wall. Then I would go into the wood and cut the thickest stick I could find and then I would come home and beat you." said Molly Whuppie.

"Then that is EXACTLY what I shall do to you," laughed the giant.

43

And he did. When he had gone into the forest to look for the thickest stick he could find, Molly Whuppie stroked the cat and dog who were in the sack with her, and sang out, in a loud voice,

"Oh, if only everyone could see what I can see!"

"What can you see?" cried the giant's wife. "Whatever it is, let me see it too."

"If you really want to," said Molly Whuppie. She took the scissors, cut a hole in the bottom of the sack, and jumped out.

"You must get inside the sack if you want to see what I saw," said Molly Whuppie.

The giant's wife climbed into the sack and Molly Whuppie sewed her in.

It was dark inside the sack.
The giant's wife didn't like it,
and cried to be let out. But
Molly Whuppie had hidden herself
and would not reply.

When the giant returned home
with the thickest stick he could
find he began to beat the sack.

"Take that! . . . and that! . . . and
that!"

"Stop! Stop! It's ME!
It's ME!" shouted the giant's wife.

The cat began to yowl. The dog began to bark. There was
so much noise the giant didn't recognize her voice at first. By
the time he realised it was his wife in the sack and NOT Molly
Whuppie, Molly Whuppie was safely over the Bridge of One Hair.
He was VERY angry at being tricked again, but there was NOTHING
he could do about it.

Molly Whuppie married the King's youngest son, and everyone,
except maybe the giant, lived happily ever after.

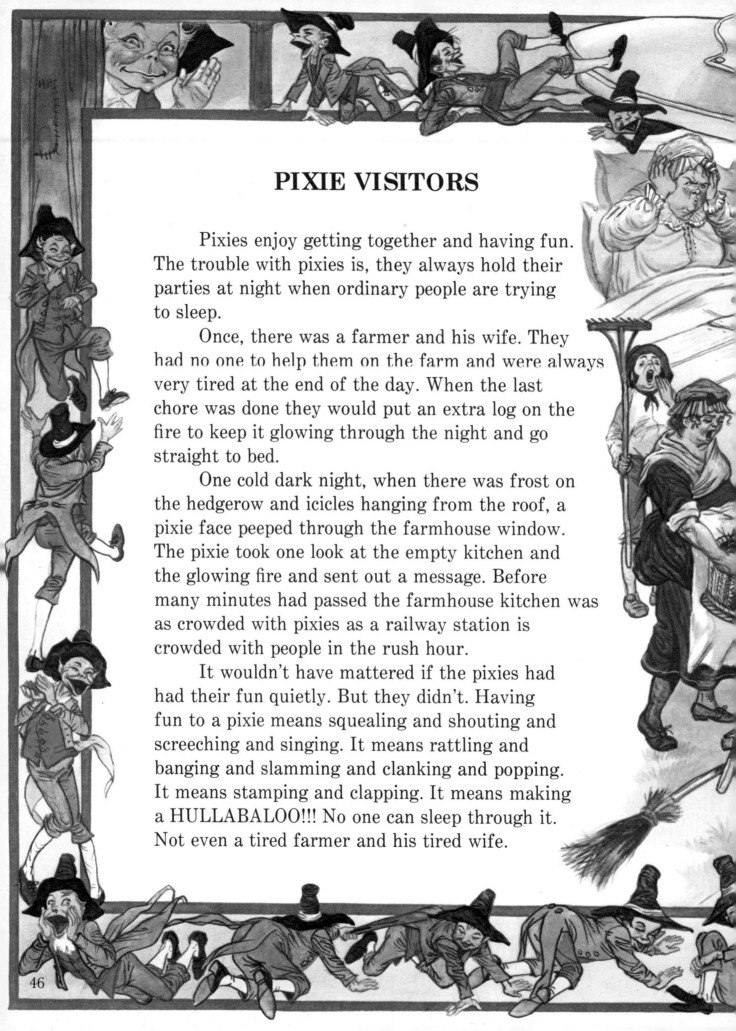

PIXIE VISITORS

Pixies enjoy getting together and having fun. The trouble with pixies is, they always hold their parties at night when ordinary people are trying to sleep.

Once, there was a farmer and his wife. They had no one to help them on the farm and were always very tired at the end of the day. When the last chore was done they would put an extra log on the fire to keep it glowing through the night and go straight to bed.

One cold dark night, when there was frost on the hedgerow and icicles hanging from the roof, a pixie face peeped through the farmhouse window. The pixie took one look at the empty kitchen and the glowing fire and sent out a message. Before many minutes had passed the farmhouse kitchen was as crowded with pixies as a railway station is crowded with people in the rush hour.

It wouldn't have mattered if the pixies had had their fun quietly. But they didn't. Having fun to a pixie means squealing and shouting and screeching and singing. It means rattling and banging and slamming and clanking and popping. It means stamping and clapping. It means making a HULLABALOO!!! No one can sleep through it. Not even a tired farmer and his tired wife.

"Who is making all that noise?" cried the farmer's wife, sitting up in bed and pressing her hands to her ears.

"There are pixies playing in the kitchen," said the farmer who was on his hands and knees peeping through a hole in the floor.

"Then tell them to go and play somewhere else," grumbled his wife.

"I can't do that," said the farmer. And he was right! He couldn't! If he offended the pixies there was no telling what they might do. There are so many things on a farm that a pixie can make go wrong. They can curdle the milk and stop the hens laying for a start. If they are really annoyed they can make EVERYTHING go wrong.

"We'll just have to put up with the noise," sighed the farmer.

The farmhouse kitchen was warm and cosy and the pixies liked it so much they began to come EVERY night. The farmer and his wife hardly slept at all. They grew more and more tired. They just couldn't stop yawning during the day. When the farmer's wife fell asleep in the hen house and dropped all the eggs she had been collecting, the farmer decided the time had come to do something. But what? Offend the pixies and they were in trouble.

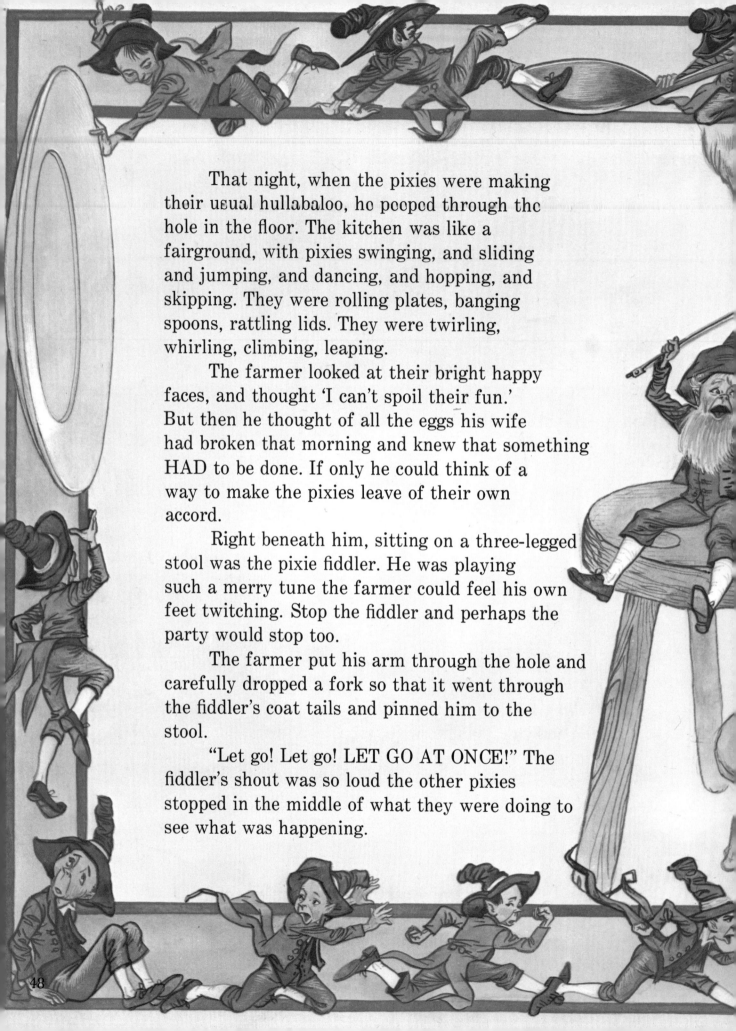

That night, when the pixies were making their usual hullabaloo, he peeped through the hole in the floor. The kitchen was like a fairground, with pixies swinging, and sliding and jumping, and dancing, and hopping, and skipping. They were rolling plates, banging spoons, rattling lids. They were twirling, whirling, climbing, leaping.

The farmer looked at their bright happy faces, and thought 'I can't spoil their fun.' But then he thought of all the eggs his wife had broken that morning and knew that something HAD to be done. If only he could think of a way to make the pixies leave of their own accord.

Right beneath him, sitting on a three-legged stool was the pixie fiddler. He was playing such a merry tune the farmer could feel his own feet twitching. Stop the fiddler and perhaps the party would stop too.

The farmer put his arm through the hole and carefully dropped a fork so that it went through the fiddler's coat tails and pinned him to the stool.

"Let go! Let go! LET GO AT ONCE!" The fiddler's shout was so loud the other pixies stopped in the middle of what they were doing to see what was happening.

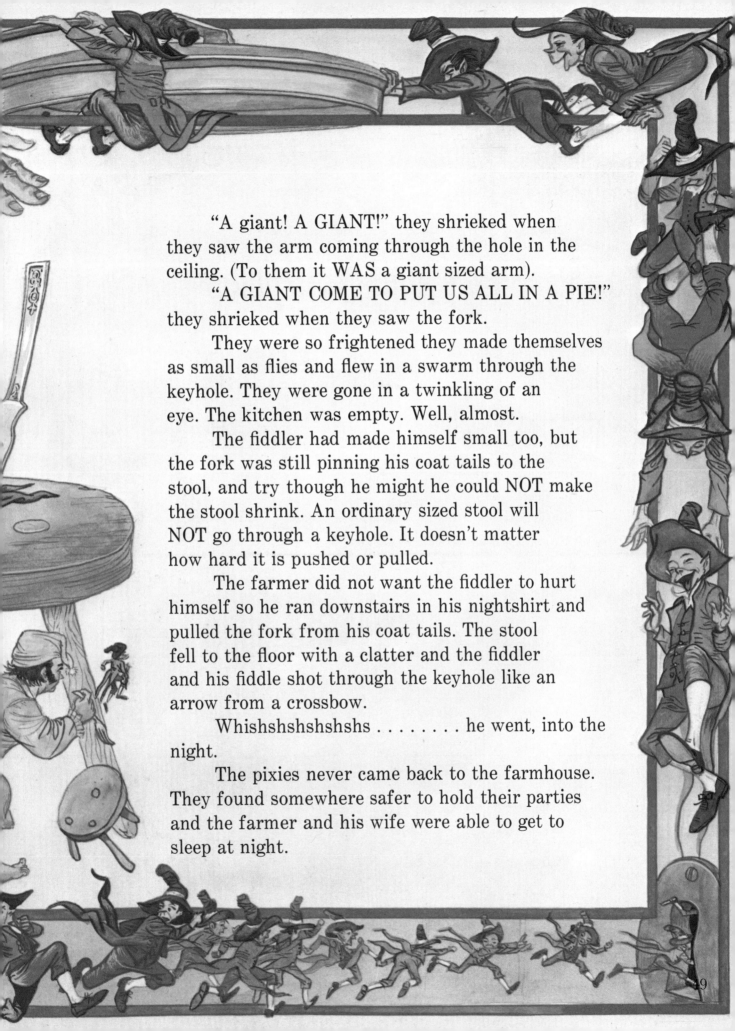

"A giant! A GIANT!" they shrieked when they saw the arm coming through the hole in the ceiling. (To them it WAS a giant sized arm).

"A GIANT COME TO PUT US ALL IN A PIE!" they shrieked when they saw the fork.

They were so frightened they made themselves as small as flies and flew in a swarm through the keyhole. They were gone in a twinkling of an eye. The kitchen was empty. Well, almost.

The fiddler had made himself small too, but the fork was still pinning his coat tails to the stool, and try though he might he could NOT make the stool shrink. An ordinary sized stool will NOT go through a keyhole. It doesn't matter how hard it is pushed or pulled.

The farmer did not want the fiddler to hurt himself so he ran downstairs in his nightshirt and pulled the fork from his coat tails. The stool fell to the floor with a clatter and the fiddler and his fiddle shot through the keyhole like an arrow from a crossbow.

Whishshshshshshs . . . . he went, into the night.

The pixies never came back to the farmhouse. They found somewhere safer to hold their parties and the farmer and his wife were able to get to sleep at night.

LONG NOSE

Once there was a miller who had three sons, and a farmer who had a pretty daughter. One day, Roland, the eldest of the miller's three sons, said, "I am going to ask Margaret to marry me today."

In the lane leading to the farmhouse he met Old Molly. She was wrinkled and bent, and very ugly. Unkind people called her Mad Molly, and said she was a witch.

"Good day!" said Old Molly. "And where might you be going?"

Roland stuck his nose in the air and walked past her as though she wasn't there. It was a wonder he didn't fall over his own feet.

"No!" said Margaret, when Roland proposed. "I will NOT marry you."

A few days later, Robert, the second of the miller's sons said, "I am going to ask Margaret to marry ME today." He was quite sure he would succeed where his brother had failed.

Old Molly was gathering primroses in the lane leading to the farmhouse.

"Good day!" she said politely. "And where might you be going?"

Robert stuck HIS nose into the air and pretended to look at a bird which wasn't there.

"No! I will not marry YOU!" said Margaret when Robert asked her to marry him.

Robin was the third, and youngest, of the miller's three sons. He was kind and strong, but he had one fault. At least HE thought it was a fault. He had a very, long nose. A very, VERY long nose – the kind of nose that people laugh at. He wanted Margaret to marry HIM.

He met Old Molly by the farmhouse gate.

"Good day!" said Old Molly. "And where are you going?"

"On a hopeless errand," sighed Robin. "How can I expect Margaret to marry me when I have such a ridiculous nose. She has refused my two brothers, she is sure to refuse me."

"That's where you're wrong!" said Old Molly. "She shall marry you." She took a ring from one of her bony fingers and gave it to him. "Put that on and say 'Bless it'," she said.

Robin put the ring on his own finger.

"Go on, say what I told you to say," said Old Molly.

"Bless it," said Robin, and straight away his nose shrank half an inch. It really was quite surprising the way it happened, and how handsome it made him look.

"If Margaret refuses to marry you," said Old Molly, "Say 'Drat it' and then HER nose will grow half an inch. It will make her so ugly she will be glad to marry you."

"Thank you," said Robin. "I'll ask her straight away."

When he got to the farmhouse Margaret was out.

"I'll wait," he said, and sat down. He began to day-dream and presently he closed his eyes.

Now, it so happened that there was another visitor at the farmhouse that day. He was an old miser who never spent a penny unless he had to. He was very rich, and Margaret's father, who thought being rich was important, wanted Margaret to marry him. The miser saw Robin sitting with his eyes closed and he saw the ring on Robin's finger.

'I'll take that, and give it to Margaret, then I will not have to spend money buying her a ring,' he thought. And very slyly, and very carefully, he took the ring from Robin's finger and slipped it onto his own for safe keeping.

Robin might have had his eyes closed, but he wasn't asleep. He knew exactly what the miser was doing. As soon as the ring was on the miser's finger he whispered, "Drat it."

"OOOH," said the miser. "Something has stung me!" He put his hand up to feel his nose, which was – you must have guessed – half an inch longer than it had been a moment before. "OOOOOH! Something is making my nose swell!"

"Drat it!" whispered Robin again. The miser's nose grew another half inch. "Drat it!" whispered Robin.

"What's happening?" shouted the miser as his nose grew even longer. "I must find a doctor at once." So away he rushed, trying to cover his nose with his hands. It wasn't easy because the end kept poking through his fingers.

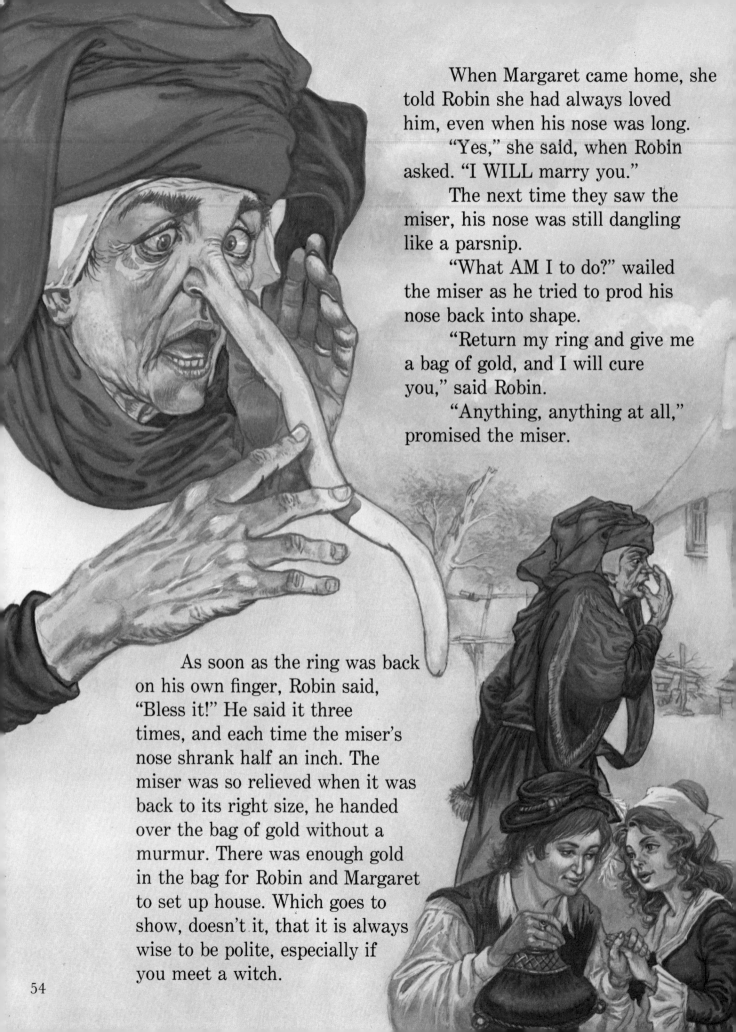

When Margaret came home, she told Robin she had always loved him, even when his nose was long.

"Yes," she said, when Robin asked. "I WILL marry you."

The next time they saw the miser, his nose was still dangling like a parsnip.

"What AM I to do?" wailed the miser as he tried to prod his nose back into shape.

"Return my ring and give me a bag of gold, and I will cure you," said Robin.

"Anything, anything at all," promised the miser.

As soon as the ring was back on his own finger, Robin said, "Bless it!" He said it three times, and each time the miser's nose shrank half an inch. The miser was so relieved when it was back to its right size, he handed over the bag of gold without a murmur. There was enough gold in the bag for Robin and Margaret to set up house. Which goes to show, doesn't it, that it is always wise to be polite, especially if you meet a witch.

54

FRENCH PUCK

French Puck was very fond of playing tricks. He never did anyone harm, but he sometimes made people feel very foolish.

One day he overheard two people talking.

"It is our wedding day a week from tomorrow," said Jeanne. "It is market day today. We must go into town and buy all the things we need to set up house."

"There will be a lot to carry," said Jules. "We must take the horse and cart."

French Puck chuckled to himself, and sat on a fence and teased some chickens to while away the time while he waited for their return. With so many things to buy they were sure to forget something.

It was late afternoon before Jeanne and Jules returned. The cart was so loaded there was barely room for them on it.

French Puck leapt through the air, light as a goose feather, and sat on a chair leg behind them.

"Have we knives?" Jeanne was asking.

"Yes."

"Have we soap?"

"Yes."

"Then we have everything we need," said Jeanne with a happy sigh, and she snuggled up to Jules and began to dream about their wedding day.

The horse was trotting. The birds were singing. Jules was whistling. Jeanne was dreaming. And French Puck was waiting. He didn't have long to wait.

Suddenly, Jeanne sat up with such a start, Jules jerked on the horse's reins, and between them they almost upset the cart.

"Oh, no," wailed Jeanne.

A gleeful grin spread across French Puck's face. He rubbed his hands together in anticipation and his pointed ears twitched.

'Ho, ho,' he thought to himself. 'She's remembered something she has forgotten.'

"Whatever made you shout out like that?" asked Jules when they had quietened the horse and made sure nothing had fallen from the cart.

"I've forgotten to buy the thread the dressmaker needs to sew my wedding clothes," sighed Jeanne.

"Is THAT all! Surely you've got thread at home," said Jules.

"Only white . . . I need pink, and the palest of yellow, and apricot and delicate sky blue, and one with a touch of green in it. We shall have to go back to town to get some."

Jules sighed. It was a long way back to town, but he supposed he would have to go. He had the cart turned half way across the road when Jeanne cried out again.

"Look! Look!"

"What now?" grumbled Jules, who had quite enough to do trying to persuade the horse to take the right direction.

"Hey! Be careful!" he cried as Jeanne jumped from the cart.

"Look! A ball of thread!" And what a ball of thread it was! It had ALL the colours in it that she needed -- pink, yellow, apricot, sky blue and delicate green.

"Oh, what a lucky thing I saw it," cried Jeanne.

"But how did it get there?" asked Jules.

"This isn't the time to be asking silly questions," said Jeanne, climbing back onto the cart.

Jules turned the cart homewards again and they continued on their way, with Jeanne carrying the precious ball of thread on her lap, and with French Puck doing somersaults on the chair leg behind them.

The dressmaker was very pleased when she saw the thre

"It's absolutely perfect," she said. She was even more pleased with it as she sewed t wedding clothes. It was as smooth as silk, it didn't break it didn't knot, and each colour was exactly the right length.

The wedding day came, and everyone, and that included French
Puck, gathered outside the church to see the new bride. How
pretty she looked.

"What a beautiful dress!" everybody exclaimed.

And then it happened! Crick! Crack! The tiny coloured
bows decorating the skirt began to float to the ground.

"Ooh!" gasped Jeanne.

"What is happening?" gasped everyone else.

Crick! Crack! The muslin flowers decorating the bodice
fell in a shower of petals.

59

Crick! Crack! The frill round the bottom of the skirt fell to the ground . . . then the skirt itself tumbled round Jeanne's ankles . . . the sleeves came apart and fell from her arms . . . the bodice fell into five different pieces.

Poor Jeanne was left standing in her petticoat, with her wedding dress in tatters around her. Someone ran from the crowd and put a cloak round her shoulders, and Jules took her home so that she could put on another dress.

"The thread I sewed with must have been rotten," said the dressmaker, who was blushing as scarlet as Jeanne herself. Oh, the shame of it all.

When everyone else had gone, she gathered the pieces together. She looked at them very carefully. She turned each piece over and over. She couldn't find one tiny piece of sewing thread anywhere. It had ALL disappeared.

"I should have known such perfect thread was too good to be true," she sighed.

The mystery was never explained, but then nobody had seen French Puck, had they?

THE BOASTFUL TAILOR

One day, a tailor who was always boasting about how clever he was, decided to go out and see something of the world. He walked a long way and at last came to a steep hill behind which he could see the tops of some trees, and a very tall tower. The tower was so tall it disappeared into a cloud.

"I'll go and see who lives there," said the tailor boldly. "I am afraid of nothing." He even boasted to himself.

He had only gone a few yards when something odd happened. The tower began to move. The tailor rubbed his eyes. Surely he must be imagining it? Towers don't move. But this one did. It stepped right over the hill and stood in front of the tailor. It wasn't a tower at all. It was a leg. A giant's leg. It was quickly followed by a second. And where there are two giant legs, there is bound to be a giant.

61

"WHAT DO YOU WANT?" bellowed the giant.

The tailor put his cupped hands to his mouth and called back, "I want to earn myself a crust of bread!"

"You may come and work for me," bellowed the giant. The tailor didn't think it was an offer he could very well refuse, since he was so small and the giant was so big.

"What wage will you give me?" he asked.

"I will give you three hundred and sixty five days every year, and an extra day every leap year," said the giant.

"That sounds fair," said the tailor, determined however, to make his escape as quickly as he could.

The first task the giant set him was to fetch water.

"Will one jugful be enough?" asked the tailor. "Or shall I bring the well? If the well isn't enough I will bring the spring too."

"No, no, the jug holds enough," said the giant. And he thought to himself. 'This is no ordinary man if he can fetch a well and a spring too. I must be careful what I say to him.'

The second task the giant set the tailor was to cut wood.

"Why not let me bring the whole forest and be done with it," said the tailor boastfully.

"No, no, there's no need to do that," growled the giant into his beard. "Fetch well and spring too . . . cut a whole forest! What sort of man is this?"

The third task the giant set the tailor was to shoot two wild pigs for their supper.

"I'll bring you a thousand," boasted the tailor.

"No, no, two will do," said the giant. And he muttered into his beard, "Fetch well and spring too . . . cut a whole forest . . . bring a thousand pigs. This man is dangerous. The sooner I am rid of him the better." He was so worried he lay awake all night trying to think of a way to get rid of the tailor.

The next morning the giant took the tailor to a marsh where willow trees grew. The giant picked up the tailor and sat him on one of the springy willow branches.

"I don't suppose even YOU can bend that branch to the ground," said the giant.

"Oh yes I can!" boasted the tailor. He took a deep breath and held it inside his chest, then he pushed at the branch. Slowly it began to bend.

"More . . . " said the giant.

The tailor pressed harder. The branch sank lower. The tailor's breath had disappeared. He needed to take a new one. He HAD to take a new one. But the instant he opened his mouth to breathe in, the springy willow branch hurled him into the air, like a catapult hurling a stone. Higher he went . . . higher and higher. He must have gone over the moon because he was never seen again, much to the giant's relief.

If the tailor hadn't been so boastful, he would probably be sitting at home now, telling his grandchildren about a giant he had once known.

THE TWO WIZARDS

Once there were three brothers. The two eldest spent all their spare time playing draughts, and the youngest spent all his time learning how to become a wizard. One day, Bertram, who already knew a thing or two about wizardry, said, to his brothers,

"I feel like having some fun. I will change myself into a horse, and you can take me into the city and sell me."

"What will happen when you are sold?" asked his brothers.

"It will be fun to find out," said Bertram.

Who should buy Bertram in his new shape as a white horse, but the King himself. He paid for him with twelve of the best elephants in the palace elephant stable.

"What are you going to do?" whispered Bertram's brothers as the King prepared to mount. "The King will behead you if he finds out you have tricked him."

"Don't worry about me," whispered Bertram. "Take the elephants and go home."

The white horse gave the King a splendid ride. No one else could keep up with him. When they arrived at the palace gate the King had to dismount to open the gate himself.

No sooner had he dismounted than the white horse bolted.

"Catch that horse! Catch that horse!" shouted the King. But by the time the grooms had mounted their horses, the white horse was nowhere to be seen.

The King sent for his own wizard.

"I paid twelve of my best elephants for that horse," he said. "You MUST find it."

The King's wizard was no fool. He knew a thing or two himself. 'Set a horse to catch a horse,' he thought, and changed himself into a black stallion.

The white horse was grazing in a field. He heard the black stallion galloping towards him, and changed himself into a large white eagle. He soared up into the sky on strong white wings.

The King's wizard, who certainly did know a thing or two, changed into a black eagle. He soared up into the sky on strong black wings.

The white eagle saw him coming and changed into a white hawk. The black eagle changed into a black kite and chased the hawk into the trees, where Bertram's brothers were sitting playing draughts.

The white hawk changed into a white draught piece and hid amongst the other pieces on the board.

The black kite changed into the King's wizard.

"May I have my draught piece?" he asked.

"These are OUR draught pieces," said Bertram's brothers.

"Count them. You will find you have one too many," said the King's wizard. Of course, when Bertram's brothers counted the pieces, they found they did have one too many.

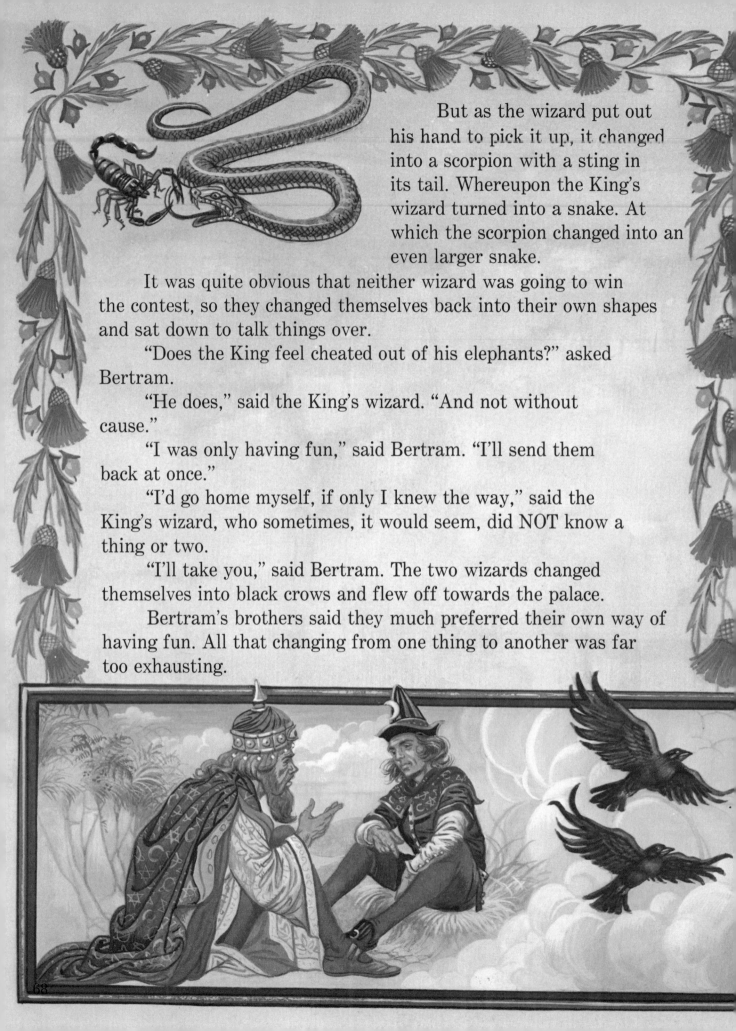

But as the wizard put out his hand to pick it up, it changed into a scorpion with a sting in its tail. Whereupon the King's wizard turned into a snake. At which the scorpion changed into an even larger snake.

It was quite obvious that neither wizard was going to win the contest, so they changed themselves back into their own shapes and sat down to talk things over.

"Does the King feel cheated out of his elephants?" asked Bertram.

"He does," said the King's wizard. "And not without cause."

"I was only having fun," said Bertram. "I'll send them back at once."

"I'd go home myself, if only I knew the way," said the King's wizard, who sometimes, it would seem, did NOT know a thing or two.

"I'll take you," said Bertram. The two wizards changed themselves into black crows and flew off towards the palace.

Bertram's brothers said they much preferred their own way of having fun. All that changing from one thing to another was far too exhausting.

SNOW-WHITE AND ROSE-RED

Once there was a woman who lived in a lonely cottage in the middle of a wood. She had two daughters, one called Snow-White, and the other Rose-Red. One winter evening, when they were all sitting by the fire, there was a knock at the door.

"Someone must be seeking shelter from the cold," said the woman and went to open the door.

Standing on the doorstep, his black fur sprinkled with snow, was an enormous bear. Snow-White and Rose-Red took one look at his bright shining eyes, and his powerful claws, and ran to hide.

"You look very cold," said the woman to the bear. "Please come in and warm yourself by the fire."

"Do not be afraid," said the bear when he saw the children peeping at him. "I will not harm you."

"Will you help me brush the snow from my fur?" asked the bear, as the children crept nervously from their hiding place. They picked up the broom so that they could brush him without getting too close, but the bear was so friendly and it was such fun brushing a bear with a broom they soon forgot to be afraid.

The bear came to the house and slept by the fire every night throughout the long winter. He and the children became firm friends, and no matter how roughly the children played, the bear was always very gentle.

Then one day, as summer grew near, the bear said goodbye.

"I must go and protect my treasure from the dwarfs," he said. "They stay underground in winter but in summer they get everywhere. I fear they are not to be trusted."

One day, later that summer, when Snow-White and Rose-Red
were in the wood picking wild strawberries, they saw a dwarf
themselves. He was jumping up and down in a terrible rage.
The end of his beard had caught in a crack in a fallen log and
he couldn't get it out.

"How did it happen?" asked Snow-White, as she and Rose-Red
did their best to pull him free.

"Not that it's any business of yours," grumbled the dwarf,
"but I was driving a wedge into the crack to keep it open. The
wedge popped out and the crack closed up again over my beard . . .
Ouch! Ouch! You're hurting me! Be careful!"

"We can't get you out on our own," said Rose-Red. "I'll go and get some help."

"I can't wait that long . . . think of something yourself," grumpled the dwarf. And so Snow-White, thinking the dwarf would be pleased, took the scissors, which she always carried in her pocket, and cut through his beard. He was free, but the tip of his beard was growing out of the log like a fuzzy white fungus. The dwarf wasn't at all pleased. He picked up the sack of gold which was lying beside the log, and stomped off, without even the hint of a thank you.

A few days later, Snow-White and Rose-Red went to the river to catch fish. Who should they see there but the very same dwarf. He was in terrible trouble. The end of his beard had caught in his fishing line, and a fish was pulling the line, and him, into the river.

"Help me! Help me!" shrieked the dwarf, holding as tightly as he could to a bunch of reeds. He was slipping all the time.

"We must do something quickly or he will drown," said Rose-Red.

Snow-White took out her scissors and snipped the end off the dwarf's beard. The dwarf fell backwards into the reeds and the fish swam away. Was the dwarf grateful? Not at all! He picked up a sack of pearls which was lying in the reeds and stomped off with a bad-tempered glare and not even a hint of a thank you.

72

Some time later, Snow-White and Rose-Red were crossing the heath when an eagle, which had been hovering over a rock, suddenly swooped low. There was a terrible cry. They ran to see what had happened. The eagle had its talons in the dwarf's coat and was lifting him from the ground.

"Help me!" shrieked the dwarf. Snow-White and Rose-Red caught hold of his legs and pulled . . . downwards. The eagle held on tight with his talons and pulled . . . upwards.

"You'll tear me in two!" shrieked the dwarf. But all that was torn was his coat, as the eagle continued to soar upwards and HE fell with a thud to the ground. Was he grateful at being rescued? No, he wasn't. "You should have been more careful, then you wouldn't have torn my coat," he grumbled. He picked up a sack of precious stones which was lying beside the rock and disappeared into a cave. Snow-White and Rose-Red were quite used to the dwarf's grumpy ways by now. They didn't expect a thank you. Which was just as well, because they didn't get one.

Later in the afternoon they caught the dwarf by surprise. He had emptied the sack of precious stones onto the ground and was gloating over their colours and their sparkle. He stamped his feet and shook his fists when he saw them. He was VERY annoyed.

"How DARE you spy on me!" he shouted. In the very middle of his rage an enormous black bear came ambling along the path.

The dwarf turned as pale as an uncooked pancake, and ran towards his cave. But the bear was quicker than he was and stood in his way.

"Don't eat me . . . please don't eat me!" The dwarf was shivering with fright. "You can have ALL my treasure! I'm too small and thin to eat! Eat those two wicked girls!"

The bear raised his paw and knocked the dwarf to the ground. Snow-White and Rose-Red were very frightened, but the bear called to them not to be afraid and they recognised his voice. As they ran to him, his bearskin fell to the ground. He wasn't a bear at all, but a king who had been bewitched by the dwarf, and the treasure the dwarf had been gloating over was his. Now the bad-tempered dwarf was dead, and the spell was broken.

MOTHER HOLLE

Once there were two step-sisters, who were as different as chalk and cheese. Martha was idle and never did a thing unless she HAD to, which wasn't very often for she was her mother's favourite. Anna was always busy. She HAD to be, for she was only a step-daughter.

One day, Anna was sitting in the garden spinning when she pricked her finger. A speck of blood fell onto the shuttle. She was trying to wash it clean when it slipped from her fingers and fell to the bottom of the well.

"YOU dropped it! YOU must go down and get it!" shouted her step-mother in such a rage that Anna had no choice but to do as she was told. She must have bumped her head as she fell, for she remembered nothing until she woke, and found herself in a pleasant field. She got to her feet and began to walk. Presently she came to an oven.

"Take me out . . . before I burn cried the bread in the oven.

Anna took the bread from the oven and set it to cool.

A little further on she came to a tree.

"Shake me!" cried the tree. "My apples are ripe!"

Anna shook the tree. When all the apples had fallen she piled them neatly, then went on her way until she came to the house of a witch.

"You must come and work for me," said the witch. "Your most important task will be to shake my feather bed every morning. I am Mother Holle. If my bed is not shaken properly there will be no snow."

Mother Holle was very kind to Anna and for a while Anna was happy, but then she began to feel homesick.

"You have worked very hard," said Mother Holle, "and I will show you the way home." She took Anna to a hidden door. "Go through," said Mother Holle, handing her the lost shuttle. As Anna stepped through the door a shower of golden rain fell all about her and clung to her hair and her clothes.

"The gold is yours," said Mother Holle. "Goodbye my dear."

The next moment Anna found herself at home. As she ran across the yard, a cockerel sitting on the fence crowed

"Cock a doodle do!

A golden girl is come to you!"

"Where have you been you bad girl!" shouted her step-mother running to the door. But when she saw the gold she quickly changed her tune. "Where did you get it? How did you get it?"

Anna told her everything that had happened.

"Martha shall have gold too," said her step-mother. "Go, sit by the well Martha, and spin. Do everything as Anna did."

Martha did not like spinning and she was in a hurry to get rich. She pricked her finger on a thorn to make it bleed. She squeezed her finger so that blood fell onto the shuttle, then she threw the shuttle into the well and jumped in after it.

Everything happened as before until Martha reached the oven.

"Take me out . . . before I burn!" cried the bread.

"And get my hands dirty! Certainly not!" snapped Martha.

"Shake me . . . my apples are ripe!" called the tree.

"What! And have one fall on my head! Certainly not!" snapped Martha, and hurried on to the witch's cottage.

"I will come and work for you," she said to Mother Holle, without waiting to be asked.

On the first day she worked well. On the second day she swept the dust under the hearth-rug and didn't bother to shake Mother Holle's mattress at all. On the third day she stayed in bed until mid-afternoon.

"It is time for you to go home," said Mother Holle.

"You must pay me first," said Martha greedily.

"Certainly, I will pay you," said Mother Holle, and led her to the hidden door. This time, instead of a shower of gold descending like rain, a shower of black pitch came pouring down. It covered Martha from head to foot. It was horrid!

"That is just payment for the work you have done," said Mother Holle sternly, and closed the door behind her.

When Martha ran sobbing across the yard to the house, the cockerel sitting on the fence crowed,

"Cock a doodle do!

A dirty girl is come to you!"

UNCAMA THE HUNTER

Uncama was a bold African hunter. He lived in a small village on the edge of the forest with his wife and baby son.

One harvest time, when the crops were ready to dig, a strange animal came into the village and rooted up all the vegetables in one of the vegetable patches. It came the following night. And the night after that. Each time it carried off another lot of vegetables.

"If somebody doesn't do something soon," said Uncama, "There will be nothing left, and we will all starve."

That night he lay in wait, and watched for the strange animal. If he could catch it, he would kill it. But though Uncama kept very quiet, the strange animal heard him breathing, and fled before Uncama had time to throw his spear.

Uncama could run like the wind and he gave chase. When the animal reached the river it ran into a deep hole at the water's edge. Uncama was a brave, and bold hunter. He didn't hesitate. He followed the animal into the hole and came to an underground country. The animal disappeared and Uncama found himself in a village amongst a tribe of savage dwarfs who attacked him.

Uncama barely escaped with his life. He ran back the way he had come followed by a hail of spears.

When he returned to the village no one seemed to recognize him. Uncama could see no one he knew either.

"Where are my friends?" he asked. "And where is my wife?"

"Which wife would that be?" asked a youth.

"Do not joke. . .the wife of Uncama of course."

"I suppose you mean the Uncama who disappeared many years ago," said the youth, and led him to an old woman, with wrinkled face and bowed shoulders. Standing beside her was a fully grown man. The man was Uncama's son. Uncama thought he had been away for less than an hour. He did not know that an hour in the underground country of the dwarfs was as long as fifty years anywhere else.

The son, who had been a baby in his mother's arms when Uncama left in pursuit of the strange animal, was now older than Uncama himself.

81

THE PIGLET AND THE GNOME

One night a thief stole a fat little piglet and put him in a sack.

The piglet squealed as he was carried away, but the sack muffled the sound of the piglet's voice and his master did not hear him.

The piglet was heavy and the thief had a long way to walk. After a while he decided to take a rest. He put the sack on the ground, then sat on the ground himself and leant against a tree. He didn't mean to go to sleep, but he made the mistake of closing his eyes, and before many minutes had passed he was snoring.

The fat little piglet did
not like being in the sack. He
squealed and fidgeted and wriggled.
He huffed and he puffed and he
squirmed. Now it so happened
that the thief had put the sack
right near a hole where a
gnome had his house. The gnome
was nearly deafened when the
piglet squealed, and nearly
tipped out of bed by all the
fidgeting and wriggling. He
went outside to see what was
causing the disturbance.

He untied the sack and looked inside.

"Hallo," he said. "What are you doing in there?"

"I've been stolen," said the piglet. "I don't like it in here. I want to go home."

"And so you shall," said the gnome who could understand pig talk perfectly well. He helped the piglet out of the sack and sent him on his way.

Then, because he liked having a bit of fun, the gnome got into the sack himself and waited for the thief to wake up, which he did, a little while later.

The thief hoisted the sack onto his shoulder and set off along a dark lane. He whistled to himself, and thought about all the things he could do with the piglet he had in his sack.

There was another gnome sitting in one of the trees in the lane. He was a friend of the gnome in the sack. He knew his friend was about because he had heard him talking to the piglet, but he couldn't see him.

"Where are you Dick?" he called.

The thief nearly jumped out of his skin. He looked all around. There was no sign of anyone, that he could see. 'I must be imagining things,' he thought. And then, before he had recovered from his fright, he heard another voice. A voice that came from just behind his right ear.

"I'm in the sack
Riding pig-a-back!"

The thief felt his hair stand on end. He thought the piglet was still in the sack. After all, hadn't he put it there himself? He dropped the sack. . .and he ran. He wanted nothing to do with a talking piglet. It would tell the whole world it had been stolen and who had stolen it.

"There goes someone who will never dare to steal another piglet," laughed the gnomes as the thief disappeared into the distance.

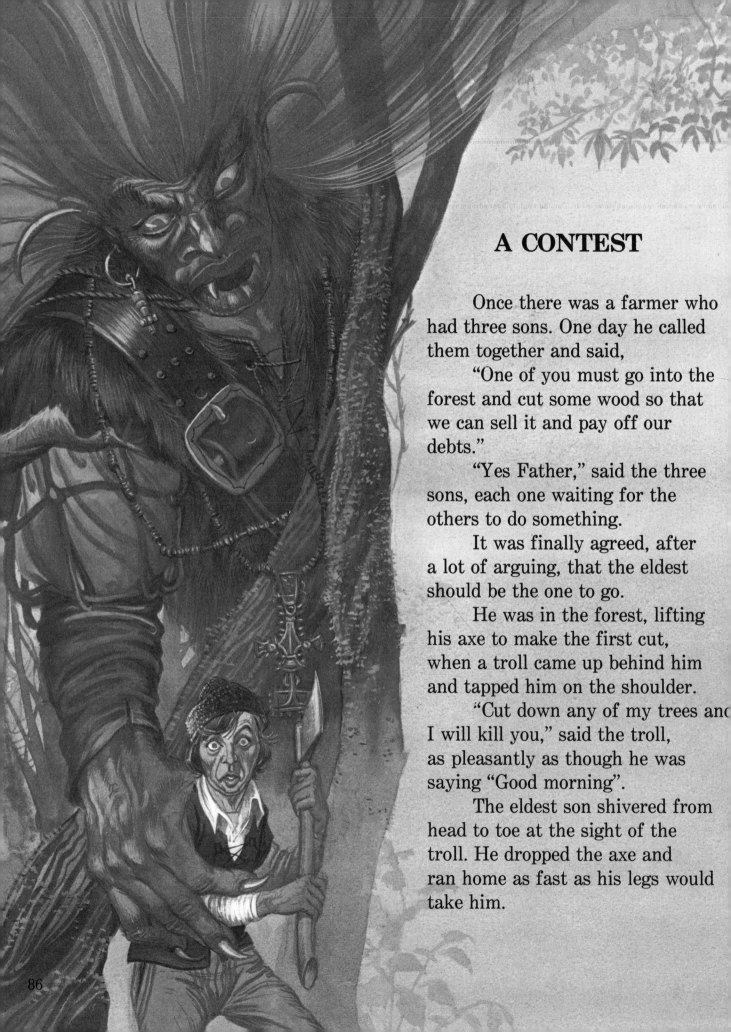

A CONTEST

Once there was a farmer who had three sons. One day he called them together and said,

"One of you must go into the forest and cut some wood so that we can sell it and pay off our debts."

"Yes Father," said the three sons, each one waiting for the others to do something.

It was finally agreed, after a lot of arguing, that the eldest should be the one to go.

He was in the forest, lifting his axe to make the first cut, when a troll came up behind him and tapped him on the shoulder.

"Cut down any of my trees and I will kill you," said the troll, as pleasantly as though he was saying "Good morning".

The eldest son shivered from head to toe at the sight of the troll. He dropped the axe and ran home as fast as his legs would take him.

"I've j-j-just s-s-seen the troll," he gasped.

"Afraid of a troll!" scoffed his father. "When I was young no troll frightened me enough to make my hair stand on end!"

On the third day, Boots, the youngest of the farmer's three sons, said he wasn't afraid of any troll and he would go into the forest.

"You!" laughed his brothers, "just you wait till you see the troll. You'll run faster than we did."

Before he set off, Boots asked his mother to make him some cheese. When it was ready, he put it in a linen bag and tied the bag to his belt.

"What! Back already?" said the farmer.

"Th-th-there's a troll in the forest."

"Afraid of a troll!" scoffed the farmer. "When I was young no troll frightened me enough to make my teeth chatter!"

The following day the second son went into the forest. He had only been gone an hour when he came running back, looking as pale as a ghost and with his hair standing on end.

Boots had sharpened his axe and was lifting it to make the first cut when someone tapped him on the shoulder. It was the troll.

"If you cut down any of my trees I will kill you," said the troll. But Boots was not as easily frightened as his brothers. Instead of running, as they had done, he took the newly made cheese from the linen bag, and squeezed it until the whey ran between his fingers. Then he looked boldly into the troll's face.

"Just you hold your tongue," he said, "or I will squeeze you as I have just squeezed this stone!"

Never, ever, in the whole of his life, had anyone dared to talk to the troll like that. Instead of flying into a rage and tearing Boots limb from limb, as you would have thought, he said meekly,

"Spare me . . . and I will help you."

By evening Boots and the troll had cut so many logs it was impossible to count them. As it began to get dark the troll said,

"My house is nearer than yours. Come and stay the night with me." It seemed a far better idea than walking all the way back through the forest and falling over things in the dark, so Boots agreed.

"Fetch some water from the stream and I will make porridge for our supper," said the troll when they got to his house. "The buckets are beside the door."

Boots had already seen them. They were big enough for him to bathe in. He might have been able to lift one when it was empty, but he certainly wouldn't be able to carry it when it was full. He had to think quickly.

"I'll bring the stream in," he called boldly. "Then you will have as much water as you need."

"You can't do that," said the troll in a panic. "Think of the mess it would make. I've got a better idea. You make up the fire and I will bring the water."

When the fire was burning brightly the troll made porridge. There was enough bubbling in the pot to keep Boots and his two brothers fed for a week.

"Let's have an eating contest," said Boots. "I'll wager I can eat more porridge than you can."

The troll looked at Boots. He looked down at himself. He looked at the pot full of thick stodgy porridge. This would be a contest he couldn't lose.

"Why not!" he said, and took two plates to the pot and filled them both to the brim. He didn't see Boots put the linen bag under his coat and arrange it with the open end under his chin.

"Let's begin," said Boots, and picked up his spoon. For every spoonful of porridge Boots put into himself, he put four into the bag under his coat. Very soon his plate was empty and the bag under his coat was bulging.

"More please," he said.

The troll was amazed. "Are you sure you've got room?" he asked, looking at what he thought was Boot's round, fat, tummy.

"Of course I have," said Boots.

"Don't you feel just a little bit full?" asked the troll doubtfully.

"No," said Boots, and without so much as a blink, or a wince, he stuck his knife through his coat and into the bag which was hidden under his coat. The bag went flat as the porridge dribbled onto the floor. "Now I've got plenty of room," said Boots, and held out his plate for another helping.

When the troll had finished his second plateful, and Boots was half-way through his third, the troll put down his spoon and sighed. "I can't eat any more," he said.

"Do as I did and make a hole in your stomach," said Boots.

"But doesn't that hurt?" asked the troll.

"Did you see me wince? Did you hear me cry out?" asked Boots. The troll had to admit that he hadn't.

And so the troll did as Boots had done, but with one big difference. He hadn't got a linen bag hidden under his coat. So that was the end of the poor old troll.

Boots took home all the silver and gold he could find and paid off his father's debts and he never ate another spoonful of porridge as long as he lived.

RAIKO AND THE GOBLIN

Raiko was one of the richest men in all Japan. He was also the meanest. He had servants to look after his house and gardeners to look after his garden. The only thing he ever gave the poor was the scent from his garden. He wouldn't have given them that if he had been able to stop the wind blowing it in their direction. On a mountain ledge overlooking the valley where he lived, there lived a goblin. The goblin had the power to listen to people's thoughts, and one day, when he was sitting on his ledge, he saw Raiko walking in his garden and listened to what he was thinking. Raiko was looking for ways to save money.

'What use is a garden to anyone?' he thought. 'No one can eat flowers, and gardeners have to be paid. I'll dismiss them. And while I'm about it I'll dismiss the servants too. Why should I pay them wages when I can live in one room and look after myself?'

Raiko made the goblin very angry for he had given no thought to what would happen to the people he dismissed. Some of them had served him and his family all their lives.

That night Raiko couldn't sleep. He felt very hot, and uncomfortable, which wasn't surprising for he kept all his gold in a belt tied round his waist. He wore it everywhere, even to bed. He tossed and turned.

'I must have a fever,' he thought. 'I need someone to look after me if I'm going to be ill. I'll wait until I'm feeling better before I dismiss the servants.'

On the third evening of his strange sickness, which didn't seem to be getting any better, he had a visitor. The visitor was dressed in a long brown robe and Raiko had the uncomfortable feeling he could see right inside his head.

"You are very ill," said the visitor, as his shadow danced across the wall in the flickering lamplight. "It's a wonder the demon's haven't come for your soul already."

Weak though he was from lack of sleep, Raiko raised himself on his elbow and shouted loudly for his servants.

"Show this man out . . . at once!" But the servants didn't come running in answer to his call, the visitor stayed.

"There is a remedy for your sickness," said the visitor, as Raiko shrank back onto his pillow. "Loosen your belt. There is famine in the valley. Use your gold to feed the poor and you will be able to sleep."

"What!" shrieked Raiko, reaching under his pillow for a knife which he always kept there. "How do you know about my gold? I won't let you steal it!" He threw the knife at the visitor with every intention of killing him. But he was weak and his aim was poor. The visitor was only scratched.

The visitor leant forward and blew out the lamp. His voice rang out in the darkness like a bell of doom. "If you take no heed of what I say then you must die!"

Raiko shrank back in terror. There was a moon shining outside and a shaft of eerie light fell across the dark room. Raiko screamed. There was a huge hairy monster, with many legs, creeping across the room towards him. It crept closer . . . and closer. Raiko screamed again. A scream full of terror and pleading. He could feel the monster's eyes burning into his very heart when his servants came bursting into the room.

"Master! Master! What is it?" they cried. Their eyes were on Raiko. They did not see the monster sink to the floor and slide from the room.

Two of the gardeners saw the trail of blood it left and followed it out of the garden and up the mountain to a small cave. Sitting in the mouth of the cave was an enormous spider.

"Tell your master to loosen his belt, or I shall come and strangle him with it," it said.

But there was no need, for on their return the gardeners found Raiko weeping with remorse. "But for my servants I would have been killed," he said. He was a changed man. He vowed to look after all those who had served him, and to give half his gold to the poor.

After that, whenever the goblin looked down at the gardeners working in the beautiful garden on the hillside and at the well-fed children playing in the valley, he would touch the tiny scar on his cheek, and smile.

THE GIANT STONES

Once there was a shepherd boy who always took his sheep to graze on a high and windy plain. On a clear day he could see for miles whichever way he looked. In one direction was the village where he lived. In another was a distant winding river. And standing right in the middle of the plain, where the wind never stopped blowing, there was a circle of giant stones. No one knew how they had got there. The village people were afraid to go near them for there were tales that they were giants who had been turned into stone as a punishment. They were the only shelter the shepherd boy had when the wind blew icy cold, or the rain swept across the plain in torrents. They cast the only shadow when the sun was scorching hot. The shepherd boy was not afraid of them. He even, in time, came to look upon them as his friends.

Living in the same village as the shepherd boy was a sorcerer who could understand the language of animals and birds. One day he overheard two birds talking outside his study window.

"Have you heard . . ." one of them was twittering. "This Midsummer Eve, at midnight, the stones on the plain will rise from their pits and go to the river to drink."

"And have you heard . . ." twittered the second bird, "that there is treasure in the pits where the stones stand?"

"And have you heard . . ." said the first bird, "that if anyone takes the treasure it will turn to dust unless they give the stones a human sacrifice in return?"

The sorcerer rubbed his hands with glee, and began to plot. The treasure was his for the taking. But what could he do about the human sacrifice? The only person in the village who had no family to ask awkward questions when he disappeared was the shepherd boy. It would have to be him.

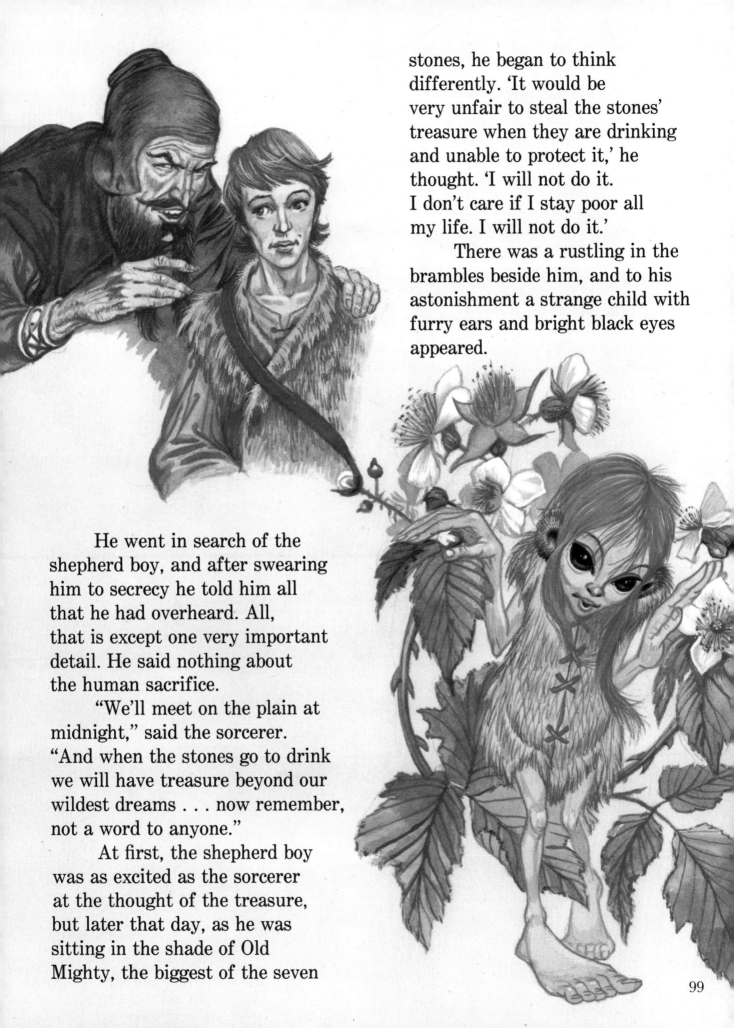

stones, he began to think differently. 'It would be very unfair to steal the stones' treasure when they are drinking and unable to protect it,' he thought. 'I will not do it. I don't care if I stay poor all my life. I will not do it.'

There was a rustling in the brambles beside him, and to his astonishment a strange child with furry ears and bright black eyes appeared.

He went in search of the shepherd boy, and after swearing him to secrecy he told him all that he had overheard. All, that is except one very important detail. He said nothing about the human sacrifice.

"We'll meet on the plain at midnight," said the sorcerer. "And when the stones go to drink we will have treasure beyond our wildest dreams . . . now remember, not a word to anyone."

At first, the shepherd boy was as excited as the sorcerer at the thought of the treasure, but later that day, as he was sitting in the shade of Old Mighty, the biggest of the seven

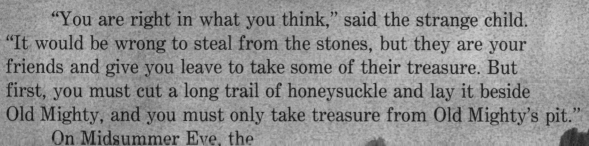

"You are right in what you think," said the strange child. "It would be wrong to steal from the stones, but they are your friends and give you leave to take some of their treasure. But first, you must cut a long trail of honeysuckle and lay it beside Old Mighty, and you must only take treasure from Old Mighty's pit."

On Midsummer Eve, the sorcerer and the shepherd boy went to the circle of stones and lay in wait for midnight. Just before the magic hour clouds covered the moon. Moments later the earth began to tremble. The stones were stepping from their pits. It was an awesome sight. Were they really enchanted giants? They began to move across the plain, rocking gently from side to side on invisible feet.

Presently there came the sound of a distant rumble. It grew louder. The stone giants were returning from the river.

'I must get out of this pit or I will be squashed under Old Mighty,' thought the shepherd boy and tried to climb out. The sides of the pit were slippery and steep. He couldn't find a foothold anywhere. He could hear the sorcerer screaming with fear.

"Quick!" cried the sorcerer, "We haven't got much time!"

The shepherd boy jumped into the pit from which Old Mighty had stepped. He gathered enough treasure to fill one of his pockets. In a nearby pit the sorcerer was shovelling treasure into sacks as fast as he could. And all the time he was shovelling he was thinking, 'No one will miss the shepherd boy . . . no one will miss the shepherd boy.'

The shepherd boy resigned himself to certain death. He looked up at the sky for the last time and saw the strange child with furry ears, peeping over the rim of the pit.

"Take hold of this," called the strange child, and lowered the trail of honeysuckle which the shepherd boy had cut and laid beside Old Mighty earlier in the day. "I will pull you up . . ."

It was a very close thing. As the shepherd boy fell gasping onto the grass Old Mighty stepped into the pit with a heavy thud. All around there were echoing thuds, and then, when the earth stopped trembling, complete silence. It was as though the stones had never moved.

The sorcerer was never seen again. The shepherd boy became a rich landowner, and though he never took sheep to graze on the plain again, he was often seen leaning against Old Mighty with a far-away look in his eyes.

MY-OWN-SELF

Peter would not go to bed when his mother told him to. He was naughty about most things, but about going to bed he was very naughty indeed.

He lived with his mother in a lonely cottage. There was nothing around it but moorland. It was a cheerful enough place during the day with bees buzzing in the heather and birds singing and twittering in the gorse bushes, but at night it was different. Sometimes it was eerie and still. Sometimes the wind seemed to be full of whispers. Peter's mother didn't like it. As soon as it was dark she would make up the fire and go to bed. She felt safe in bed. If anything happened, (it never had, but she was never certain it wouldn't) she could put her head under the blankets and pretend she wasn't there.

"It's time for bed, Peter," she would say as she put fresh logs on the fire.

"Time for you maybe, but not time for me," he would say cheekily. And he would stay up until he wanted to go to bed. Sometimes he stayed up half the night.

103

One night the wind was whispering round the house and Peter's mother felt sure there were fairies about.

"Time for bed, Peter," she said, even earlier than usual.

"Time for you, but not for me," Peter said. She pleaded. She grumbled. She shouted. Nothing she said made any difference. Peter sat toasting his toes in front of the fire and refused to move. At last she lost her temper.

"Well, I'm going to bed," she said, and she went.

Peter heard the bed creak as she got into it, and then the house fell silent, except for the crackling and spitting of the logs burning on the fire, and then that stopped too.

Presently there was a fluttering in the chimney . . . and an elf child jumped down onto the hearth.

"What's your name?" asked Peter, not in the least afraid, though he had never met an elf face to face before.

"My-Own-Self," said the elf child. "What's yours?"

"Just My-Own-Self too," said Peter, thinking if an elf child could give a funny answer, then so could he.

"I've come to play," said the elf child.

"Oooh good!" said Peter. "Now I can stay up all night."

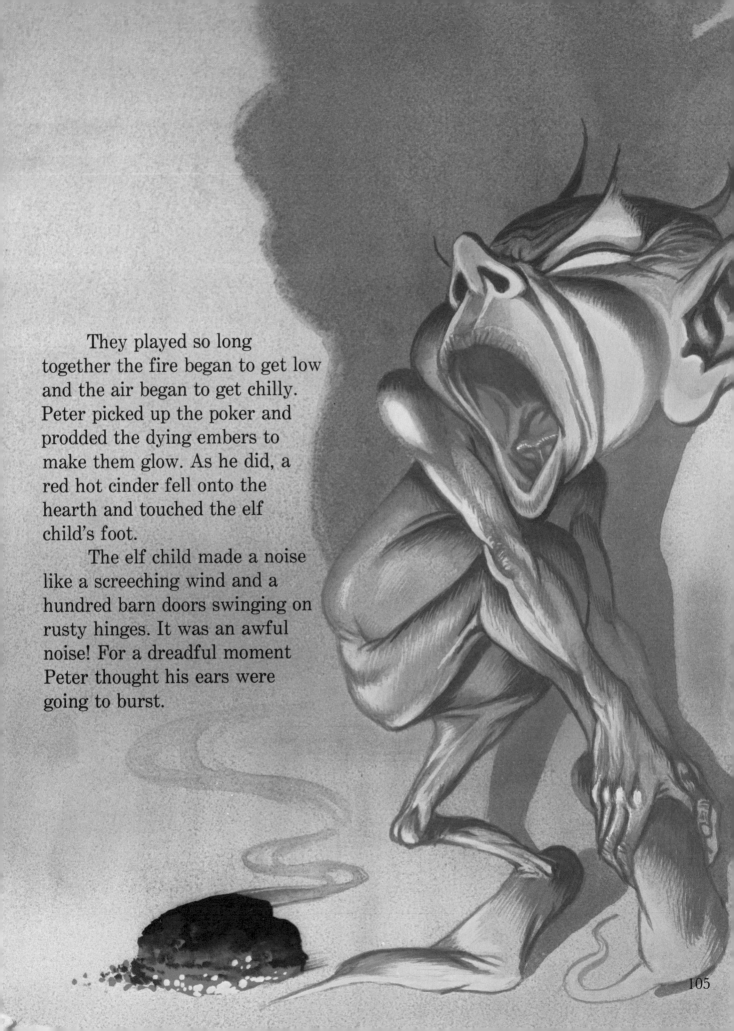

They played so long together the fire began to get low and the air began to get chilly. Peter picked up the poker and prodded the dying embers to make them glow. As he did, a red hot cinder fell onto the hearth and touched the elf child's foot.

The elf child made a noise like a screeching wind and a hundred barn doors swinging on rusty hinges. It was an awful noise! For a dreadful moment Peter thought his ears were going to burst.

Peter felt, rather than heard, that someone, something, was coming down the chimney in answer to that dreadful scream. He dived under the bed and crouched as close to the wall as he could.

"Who is there? What is wrong?" called a voice.

"It's My-Own-Self, and my foot's burnt!" cried the elf child.

"Who did it?" asked the voice angrily. Peter knew he had. He could see the angry face of an elf mother looking from the chimney.

"Just-My-Own-Self-Too" said the elf child, meaning Peter.

"If you did it yourself stop making a fuss," said the elf mother, not understanding at all. She reached out and caught hold of the elf child by his ear and yanked him up the chimney.

Peter crouched under the bed all-night long, afraid to come out. Next evening, when his mother said "Time for bed, Peter," he went straight away. He was afraid the elf mother might discover who 'Just-My-Own-Self-Too' really was, and come looking for him.

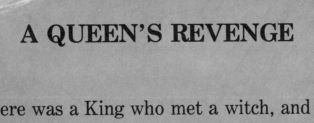

A QUEEN'S REVENGE

Once there was a King who met a witch, and married her, without knowing she was a witch. On the day he brought her home everyone gathered on the palace steps to greet her.

"How beautiful the new Queen is," they whispered.

The Queen curtsied, and smiled graciously. She knew she was beautiful. It was only right that everyone else should think so too. But as she swept into the palace on the arm of the King she heard one of her own gentlemen-in-waiting whisper,

"Look at the King's daughter. She is even more beautiful than the Queen." Little did he know what he had done.

The new Queen took the Princess by the hand and kissed her on the cheek. "You and I are going to be friends," she said with a pretty smile, but in her heart she was already plotting revenge. She wanted no rivals. That night, when everyone was asleep, she cast a spell.

Early next morning the palace echoed with loud screams. The maidservants who had gone to help the Princess to dress were running about, weeping and wailing and wringing their hands.

"What is it . . . what is it?" cried the King, who had come running in with his crown all askew.

The weeping maidservants pointed to the Princess's room.

What a dreadful sight met the King's eyes when he entered. Lying on the Princess's bed, with its head on the pillow was an ugly, scaley monster. There was no sign of the Princess herself. The poor King fell into a swoon, and while the maidservants did their best to revive him, the monster crawled unnoticed, from the bed, and from the palace. It dragged itself to distant rock and there it stayed.

The countryside was soon in terror, for hunger drove the monster to devour everything that crossed its path. When a wizard was consulted he said, "Tell the King to give the monster the milk from seven cows every day to appease its hunger . . . and tell the King his daughter will not be avenged until his son returns." The King's son was hundreds of miles away on an expedition, but the news travelled fast and when he heard what had happened the Prince swore to avenge his sister. He and his men built a long boat, with a special keel made from an ash tree, and set course for home.

108

The Queen's magic powers warned her that the Prince was coming. She summoned her imps. "Raise a storm!" she ordered. "Sink the boat! The Prince must not set one foot on land!"

The imps raised a storm which made the fish think there had been an underwater earthquake, but it made no difference to the long boat. Its ash keel protected it from the imps' magic and it rode the rough sea as though it was on a calm mill pond.

"I'm not beaten yet!" cried the Queen, when the imps reported back to her. And she cast a spell that made the monster go to the harbour entrance.

"The very person he has come to avenge shall be the cause of his death," she laughed cruelly.

The long boat was just pulling into the harbour when the monster lashed the sea with its tail and drove it back the way it had come. Each time the long boat drew close to the harbour the monster drove it back . . . again. . . and again. . . and again. The men in the long boat grew exhausted in their fight to reach the shore and at last the Prince ordered them to put back to sea.

The Queen, who had been watching the struggle, laughed, and went back to the palace where she pretended to be full of concern for the missing princess.

"What a comfort you are to me in my sorrow," sighed the King, who had been completely deceived.

The Queen wouldn't have smiled so prettily if she had known that instead of going right out to sea the long boat had gone round into the next bay. With no imps, and no monster to hinder them they landed easily. The Prince drew his sword, determined to find the monster and kill it.

"It tried to keep me from my sister," he said. "It shall die."

But the moment the Prince set foot on land, the Queen's power over the monster vanished, and when the Prince found it, instead of putting up a fight, it lay quietly on the ground. The Prince raised his sword and was about to plunge it into the monster's neck, when it spoke, with his sister's voice.

"Give me kisses three.
Though I am a poisonous worm
I will not harm thee."

'This is some trick,'
thought the Prince, and would
have struck the death blow there
and then, but before he could
strike, the monster spoke again.

"Give me kisses three.
Though I am a poisonous worm
I will not harm thee."

The Prince hesitated, then
quickly kissed its cheek. The
third time he kissed it, there
was a soft hiss and the monster
turned into his sister. He had
broken the spell.

What a joyful procession it
was back to the palace. How
gladly the King greeted his two
children.

"Now we are a family again,"
he said, turning to the Queen.

"My dear, what is wrong?"
he asked, when he saw how pale
she was.

"Watch this, Father," said
the Prince. He touched the
cowering Queen with a magic
ash twig, against which a
witch has no power, and she
shrank and shrivelled until
she became a fat ugly toad.
So then the King knew he had
been deceived and banished
her from his kingdom for ever.

THE SPIRIT IN THE BOTTLE

Once there was a woodcutter who worked and saved all he could so that he could send his son William to school. But times were hard and the day came when all the money he had saved was spent and his son had to return home.

"Do not worry, Father," said William. "I will come into the forest with you and help you cut wood. We will be able to earn enough to keep ourselves."

"How can you help me?" sighed the woodcutter. "You are not used to such work . . .besides, I've only one axe. We are far too poor to buy another."

"We'll ask our neighbour to lend us one of his until I can earn enough to buy one of my own," said William.

The next day they went into the forest together. William was young and the work was new to him. He enjoyed every minute of it, and whistled and sang as merrily as any bird.

At midday the woodcutter said, "Time to rest."

"I'm not a bit tired," said William. So while his father sat under a tree and dozed, he went in search of birds' nests.

113

William climbed trees, looked in bushes and spied on birds sitting in their nests without disturbing any of them. He was looking for a way to climb into the branches of an ancient oak when he heard a voice calling, "Let me out! Let me out!"

"Where are you? Who are you?" called William, looking about and seeing no one.

"I'm at the foot of the tree," answered the voice. "Please let me out."

William poked about amongst the grass and dried leaves, and found a dirty glass bottle lying between two gnarled roots. He rubbed it clean on his sleeve. Sitting hunched inside it, with its knees under its chin was a tiny frog like creature.

"Hallo!" said William. "What are you doing in there?"

"Let me out and I'll tell you," it shouted, banging on the side of the bottle with its tiny fist.

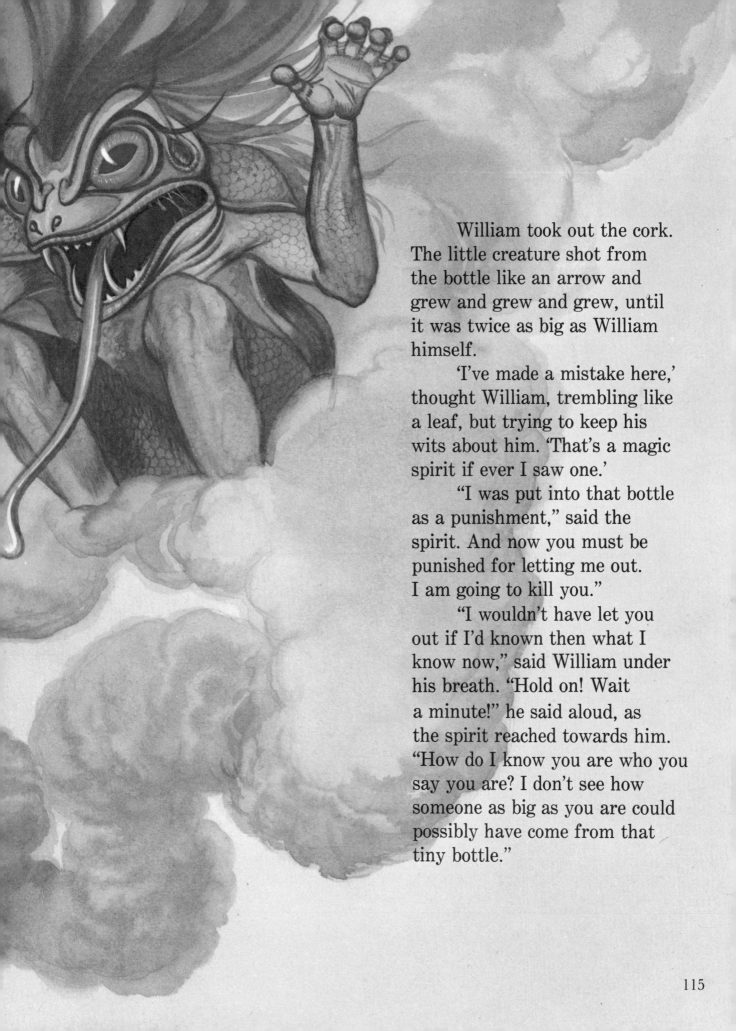

William took out the cork. The little creature shot from the bottle like an arrow and grew and grew and grew, until it was twice as big as William himself.

'I've made a mistake here,' thought William, trembling like a leaf, but trying to keep his wits about him. 'That's a magic spirit if ever I saw one.'

"I was put into that bottle as a punishment," said the spirit. And now you must be punished for letting me out. I am going to kill you."

"I wouldn't have let you out if I'd known then what I know now," said William under his breath. "Hold on! Wait a minute!" he said aloud, as the spirit reached towards him. "How do I know you are who you say you are? I don't see how someone as big as you are could possibly have come from that tiny bottle."

"Oh, don't you!" said the spirit. "Then I'll prove to you that I did." Whereupon he shrank to his former size and crawled back into the bottle.

"Got you!" shouted William and pushed the cork in.

"Let me out!" shouted the spirit in a fury. "LET ME OUT!"

"I'm not silly," said William. "If I let you out you will kill me."

"No I won't . . . I promise I won't," said the spirit. "Please, let me out."

William knew he was taking a risk, but he decided to chance his luck. He held the bottle at arm's length and took out the cork. The spirit was so grateful to be free again it gave William a piece of cloth that had the power to heal any wound, and turn iron and steel into silver.

When William returned his father said crossly,

"You will be far too tired to work this afternoon."

"I'm not tired at all," said William, and secretly rubbed the axe with the magic cloth. It turned the blade to silver, but silver isn't sharp like steel and the first blow he struck with it turned the edge up.

"Now look what you have done you foolish boy!" cried his father. "You have damaged our neighbour's axe. Now I shall have to pay for a new one."

When they got home William said he would ask the blacksmith if the axe could be repaired, but instead of going to the blacksmith he went to the silversmith. The silversmith gave him a small bag of gold in exchange for the axe.

When William next saw his father, he said, "Ask our neighbour how much he will take for his axe."

"I already have," sighed his father. "It's more than I have."

"Give him twice what he asks," said William, and showed his father the bag of gold.

And then, William told his father about the bottle he had found in the wood and the gift the spirit had given him. From that day, William and his father lived in comfort and because William used the magic cloth wisely, he became a very famous doctor.

ONCE THERE WAS A FOREST

A giant can change the look of a place as suddenly as any earthquake. Once there was a forest. It stretched for miles and miles beside the sea. It was home to many shy, wild creatures, and to two giants, though it was little more than a thick carpet to them.

Though giants are big, and strong, there is always someone, somewhere, who is brave enough to challenge them to a contest.

One of the giants who lived in the forest was tired of being challenged. He wanted to be able to eat his breakfast in peace, without having to get up every five minutes to answer the door to another Jack-the-Giant-Killer.

One day he said to his wife, "Wife, we are going to build ourselves a stronghold."

"Are we?" answered his wife with a sigh that nearly blew the birds out of the trees. Any plan of her husband's usually meant a lot of hard work for her.

"We will build it with white granite," said the giant.

"Where in the world will we get white granite from?"

"From the quarry on the far side of the forest."

"And who will carry the granite from there to here?" asked the giant's wife, though she knew the answer already.

"You will of course. I shall be busy building."

"Can't we build it with greenstone? There's plenty of that right here, and besides, it's not so heavy."

"I want my stronghold built with white granite!" said the giant with a scowl that made his wife think of sour lemons, and told her clearer than any words that it was no use arguing.

It takes a lot of anything to build a stronghold big enough to protect a giant, and granite is very heavy.

The giant's wife trudged backwards and forwards across the forest carrying boulders in her apron and getting more and more tired with each step. Backwards and forwards. Backwards and forwards. The giant built boulders into walls far quicker than she could carry them . . .after all, he only had to put one boulder on top of another.

"How slow you are!" he kept saying.

"I'm tired."

"How can you be tired? I'm not tired."

"That's because you have time to doze," she grumbled. .

"That's because I get my work done quickly."

"You're not walking as much as I am."

"Stop complaining! Walking is easier than building."

"You wouldn't say that if you were doing it." The giant's wife thought it most unfair.

The next boulder she brought was very awkward. It made her arms ache and she was afraid it would tear her apron. She had already torn the hem of her skirt and scratched her ankle on a dead tree. When she heard the giant snoring like a swarm of giant bees, she thought, "He'll never notice if I get greenstone and put it amongst the granite."

She was tiptoeing past him with an enormous greenstone boulder hidden in her apron when he woke.

"That's greenstone you've got in your apron!" he shouted, jumping up in a rage. "I suppose you thought I wouldn't notice. Take THAT for being lazy!" He lifted his foot and kicked her. She stumbled! Her apron string broke! The greenstone boulder fell! It was so huge, and it fell with such a thud, it made a hole into which the whole forest fell.

"Now look what you've done!" grumbled the giant as water swirled in from the sea and filled the hole. "You've made my feet wet!"

"Serves you right!" said his wife.

YALLERY BROWN

One night, when the moon was shining and stars were twinkling, Tom went for a walk across the moor. It was so quiet he could hear the rabbits whispering in their burrows. Presently he heard another sound. Someone was crying. It sounded like a baby. Tom searched amongst the bushes and could find nothing, and then he heard a voice saying,

"Oooh, the stone! The great big stone! Oooh, the stone is on top of me!"

"That's no baby," thought Tom. He poked about in the grass with a stick and came upon a large flat stone half hidden by weeds and moss. He felt afraid, but he just had to look underneath it. It was very heavy, and very awkward, but at last he managed to pull it up onto its end.

Underneath the stone was a scooped out hole, and lying on his back in the hole was a tiny little man. His wrinkled skin was as brown as a nut, and he had long, shining yellow hair. He blinked as the moonlight shone onto his face, then got to his feet.

Tom stood and stared.

"Close your mouth," said the little man in a voice that sounded as old as the world itself. "There's no need to be afraid. I will not hurt you. You've been kind enough to help me and so I shall help you."

"Wh.wh.who are you?" gasped Tom.

"I am Yallery Brown," said the little man. "Now for your reward. Would you like a wife to look after you?"

"I have a mother to look after me," said Tom. "But I would like some help with my work."

"Very well," said Yallery Brown. "But remember this. If you ever thank me for anything I do, I will disappear, and you will never see me again. Call 'Yallery Brown. . .come from the moors. . . I want thee', if you need me for anything, and I will come."

Before Tom could answer Yallery Brown blew a puff of dandelion seeds into his face, and when Tom could see again, Yallery Brown had gone.

Next day, Tom's work was done for him. The stables were swept. . .the horses groomed. . .the buckets filled. Whatever the master told Tom to do was done before Tom could lift a finger.

"Now I can laze in the sun whenever I want to," said Tom. He climbed to the top of the haystack and lay on his back and watched the clouds float by.

It wasn't long before the other stable boys noticed Tom was always walking around with his hands in his pockets. They couldn't understand how he was getting his work done so quickly.

Tom never actually saw Yallery Brown doing the work he was supposed to be doing, but sometimes, at night, he thought he saw him flitting about in the shadows, looking just like a shadow himself.

Lazing in the sun, doing nothing at all, tends to get boring after a time, even for someone as lazy as Tom, and one day he decided he would do some sweeping. He picked up the yard broom. It jumped from his hands. . . and swept the yard by itself.

He tried to fill the buckets. They went to the tap and filled themselves.

When he tried to push the wheelbarrow it ran away from him and wheeled itself across the stable yard.

Tom was beginning to find it all a bit scary. . .and so were the other stable boys. There were invisible hands at work. They didn't like it. They went to their master and told him what they had seen. He didn't like it either. He said Tom must leave and find work elsewhere.

"I'll never get work anywhere all the time Yallery Brown is helping me," grumbled Tom, who by this time really did want to work. "YALLERY BROWN!" he shouted. "COME FROM THE MOORS! I WANT THEE!" He felt someone tweek his leg. He spun round on his heels. There was Yallery Brown, looking up at him, and grinning all over his nut-brown face.

"I'll thank you to leave me alone Yallery Brown!" shouted Tom. "I don't want anymore of your help."

"Ho, ho," laughed Yallery Brown. "You thanked me. . .I told you not to."

"Go away! Go away! I don't care if I don't see you again!" shouted Tom, stamping his foot in a fit of temper, and not a bit grateful for all the help Yallery Brown had given him.

Yallery Brown stopped
smiling. "And now I will tell
you something else," he said
sternly. "I said, if you
thanked me you would never see
me again, and nor you shall. . .
but. . ." Tom's heart sank.
There was something about the
way Yallery Brown said 'but'
that he didn't like. ". . .but
I didn't say I would leave you
alone. With me as a friend
you could have done anything,
but you have behaved foolishly
and I shall treat you like a
fool."

Tom wanted to run, but his
legs wouldn't move. Yallery
Brown began to circle round him.
Faster . . . and faster he went,
till his yellow hair wrapped
itself round him like a scarf
and then he spiralled into the
air like a dandelion seed caught
in the wind and disappeared.

From that day onwards nothing went right for Tom. Although
he never saw Yallery Brown again, Tom knew it was Yallery Brown's
invisible hands that were responsible for all the mischief.

"If only . . ." he used to sigh. "If only I had left that
stone unturned." But by then, of course, it was too late.

127

DIGGING FOR FISH

One starry night, when the fishermen were getting their boats ready to go out to sea, an old woman hobbled along the beach towards them pulling a spindly-legged boy by the hand.

"What do you want old woman?" asked the fishermen. "Can't you see we are busy? We don't want to miss the tide."

"Take my boy with you and teach him how to fish," she said.

The fishermen took one look at the boy, who had arms like broomsticks, and laughed out load.

"You can't be serious," they guffawed. "Him. . .a fisherman! A fisherman has to battle with the sea. HE couldn't do battle with a kitten."

"Please. . ." said the boy. "I'm stronger than I look."

"Get out of our way," they said roughly. "We haven't time to waste on the likes of you."

The boy picked up one of the nets lying on the sand.

"Leave that alone!" shouted the owner and cuffed the boy's ear.

"Take the boy home old woman," jeered the fishermen. "Fishing is mens work. . .leave it to the men."

"Mens work is it!" screeched the old woman. "Well, you'll catch no fish till you bring me that!" And she pulled off the silver thimble she was wearing on her thumb and threw it onto the sand.

One of the fishermen bent to pick it up. His fingers would not close round it. It was burying itself in the sand.

It was at that awful moment the fishermen realised what they had done. They left their nets and their boats and began to dig into the sand with their hands.

"Have pity on us. . ." they pleaded. "Have pity on us. . ."

But their pleas were in vain. They are digging to this day. Their boats are neglected and falling to pieces. Their nets are tangled and rotting. All because they dared to laugh at a witch and jeer at her son.

THREE GOLDEN HAIRS

Once there was a poor man whose only son was born under a lucky star. It was foretold that, one day, he would marry the King's daughter.

The King was very cross when he heard the news. "A poor boy like that, marry my daughter! NEVER!" he said. He went to see the boy's father.

"I want to buy your son," he said.

The King was told the boy was not for sale, but he nagged, and argued, and pleaded, till at last the boy's father thought, 'My son can come to no harm with the King. He will give him a better life than I can. . .I must let him go.'

The King carried the baby off. But instead of taking him home to the palace, he put him in a box and cast the box adrift on the river. With any luck it would float out to sea and the baby would never be seen again. Marry his daughter indeed!

The boy hadn't been born under a lucky star for nothing. The box was fished from the river by a miller. He took the baby home to his wife and they brought him up as their own son. He grew into a fine strong lad, full of mischief, but kind too.

One day, the King happened, just by chance, to call at the mill.

"What a handsome boy," said the King. "Is he your son?"

"Oh that he was," sighed the miller fondly. "We found him, as a baby, floating down the river in a box."

The King went pale. He called for pen and paper and quickly wrote a letter which he sealed with bright red wax.

"Can you spare the boy to carry this letter to the Queen?" he asked the miller. "It is very urgent."

"Jack will be honoured to carry your letter," said the miller, little knowing that the King had written 'Kill the bearer of this letter. Will explain when I get home.'

Jack set off immediately. Towards nightfall he knocked at a cottage door and asked for shelter for the night.

"This is the home of a band of robbers," said an old woman who answered. "Are you sure you want to stay?"

"I am carrying a letter to the Queen. They will not harm me," said Jack. He was asleep when the robbers returned so he did not see them open the letter.

"Look at this!" they said. "Now isn't that just disgraceful. Kill a nice lad like that . . . we'll soon settle this." They wrote a new letter which said, 'Marry the bearer of this letter to our daughter', and fixed the King's seal so that it looked as though it had never been broken. They burnt the letter the King had written.

Jack continued his journey next day without knowing that the letter had been changed. He was very pleased to marry the Princess when the Queen arranged it.

When the King returned and found he had a new son-in-law he was very angry. "If you want to stay married to my daughter you must bring me three golden hairs from the head of the giant," he thundered, thinking secretly that the giant would soon put an end to Jack.

Jack set off at once. The guard at the gate of the first city he passed through asked him if he knew why the fountain in the market place had run dry. "I will give you an answer when I return," said Jack. The guard at the gate of another city asked Jack if he knew why a tree which had once borne golden apples no longer bore even a leaf. "I will have an answer for you when I return," said Jack.

The ferryman who took him across the lake asked how he could escape from the ferryboat and gain his liberty. Once again, Jack said he would give an answer on his return.

When Jack reached the giant's cave, the giant was not at home. "What do you want from him?" asked the giant's grandmother.

"Nothing very much," said Jack boldly. "Just three golden hairs from his head."

The giant's grandmother frowned. "That could be very risky," she said. "I'd better help you. But first you must hide." She turned Jack into an ant and hid him in her apron.

While they were waiting for the giant to come home Jack asked the grandmother if she knew why the city fountain had run dry.

"I do not," she said, "But I'll ask the giant if he knows."

"Will you also ask him why the tree which used to bear golden apples bears them no longer, and what the ferryman must do to gain his liberty?" asked Jack.

"I can smell boy!" said the giant when he got home. "Where is he?" But Jack was well hidden and the giant wanted his supper so he soon gave up looking.

After he had eaten the giant lay his head in his grandmother's lap and went to sleep. It wasn't long before he was snoring.

The grandmother tweeked one of the golden hairs from the giant's head.

133

"What was that?" cried the giant, waking up with a start.

"Nothing dear," said the giant's grandmother. "I was dreaming of a fountain which has run dry. Why would a fountain run dry dear?"

"Because there is a toad sitting under it," said the giant who knew the answer to almost everything. "Kill the toad and the water will flow again."

As soon as the giant closed his eyes the giant's grandmother tweeked out another of his hairs.

"Ouch!" cried the giant. "What was that?"

"Nothing dear," said the giant's grandmother. "I had another dream, that was all. Now why should an apple tree that used to bear golden apples bear them no longer?"

"There is a mouse gnawing at the root. Kill the mouse and the tree will bear fruit again," yawned the giant sleepily.

The giant's grandmother thought it better to wait a while before she pulled out the third hair.

"Ouch!" said the giant when she did. "I suppose you've had another dream?"

"Yes, I have. How did you guess?" she asked. "Now tell me, what must the ferryman do to gain his liberty?"

"Give the rudder to another passenger of course," sighed the giant. "Now will you let me get some sleep?"

"Of course dear. I won't disturb you again, I promise," she said.

The next day, when the giant's grandmother had turned Jack into himself, he set off for home.

Jack waited until he was safely across the lake before he told the ferryman how he could gain his liberty and when he answered the questions the city guards had asked, he was richly rewarded with gold and silver.

The King had to smile and pretend to be pleased when he saw Jack, for not only had Jack brought the three hairs, he was now very rich. The Princess really was pleased to see him.

It so happened that the King himself was the next person to cross the lake. The ferryman handed him the rudder. The King is ferrying passengers to this day, which probably serves him right. Perhaps, one day, Jack will tell him what he told the ferryman.

PIXIE OINTMENT

Once there was a fisherman and his wife who were friendly with the pixies. The pixies never teased them, or plagued them as they did other people. Whenever the fisherman and his wife did the pixies a favour they were handsomely rewarded.

"The pixies must be very rich," said the fisherwife. "I wonder how they come by their money."

"You might well ask," said her husband. "There's more goes on around here than meets the eye."

One night, some pixies brought a sick pixie baby to the fisherman's cottage.

"Please nurse our baby until he is well again," they said, handing the tiny bundle to the fisherwife. It was the first time either of them had seen a pixie baby. One of the pixies gave the fisherwife a small box.

"What's this?" she asked, taking a peep inside.

"It's ointment for the baby's eyes," he said. "Put a little on his eyelids every morning. Be sure not to forget. It's very important."

"I won't forget," she said.

"A word of warning," said the pixie. "If you put any of the ointment on your own eyes you will go blind."

"Ooooh! I wouldn't do a thing like that," said the fisherwife. "I'm surprised you should think such a thing."

136

"We'll come back for the baby in a few days," said the pixie. "Make sure you remember what I said."

"I will," said the fisherwife. She made the pixie baby a cradle from a pie dish, and tucked it round with thistledown to keep it warm.

On the second morning, when she had put the ointment on the baby's eyelids, she couldn't resist dabbing a little on her own.

"What are you doing?" cried her husband in alarm. "You know what the pixie said."

"Well, say it he might have done, but it hasn't made a scrap of difference to me," said the fisherwife. "I can see just as well now as I could before. You worry too much, husband. The pixies wouldn't harm me."

"How can you be so sure?" said her husband, looking very worried. "There's more goes on around here than meets the eye. . . you mark my words."

"Don't be such an old fuss pot," laughed the fisherwife.

The sick baby was soon well again. When the pixies came to take it home they asked for the box of ointment.

"Did you put any on your own eyes?" asked one pixie who took the baby.

"No! No, of course I didn't," said the fisherwife as though butter wouldn't melt in her mouth. Her husband gasped.

"Then we'll bid you good day," said the pixies.

"What nice little folk they are," said the fisherwife when they had gone.

"There's more goes on around here than meets the eye," said her husband looking very glum. "You mark my words!"

"I do wish you would stop saying that," said the fisherwife irritably.

Next market day, the fisherwife met her sister at the crossroads and they went into town.

"Isn't it busy today?" said the fisherwife.

"No more busy than usual," said her sister.

"No wonder," said the fisherwife. "The pixies are here. I've never seen them at market before. Oh, oh, the rascals! They are taking things and not paying for them! They are stealing! Did you see that! That was wicked! Did you see him take a coin from that purse?"

"I don't know what you're talking about," said her sister. "Pixies! What pixies? I see no pixies! You are imagining things!"

"I'm not! Look! you must have seen that! And that . . . and that . . ." The fisherwife spun around on her heels pointing in all directions. Suddenly she pounced on the pixie who had brought the pixie baby to the house. "You rascal!" she said, wagging her finger at him crossly. "Just you put those apples back!"

"Who are you talking to?" asked her sister, looking very bewildered.

"She cannot hear us, or see us, and you shouldn't be able to either," said the pixie. "You lied when you said you had put no ointment on your own eyes. I warned you. You should not have meddled in what doesn't concern you." He blew on her face. The fisherwife, who had seen more than she should have seen, could see nothing at all. Then she wished she had listened to her husband's words.

THE CHASE

In Iceland there once lived an old man and an old woman who were very poor. They had part of a cottage to live in, and a piece of a field to grow things in. They had one son called Karl, and one cow called Bu-cola, and that was all.

One morning, when the old woman went to milk Bu-cola she could not find her. She had disappeared without trace. There wasn't so much as a hoof mark to show which way she had gone.

"Oh, Bu-cola, where are you?" sobbed the old woman. "We shall starve without your milk."

Karl wiped his mother's tears away with the end of her apron.

"Do not cry," he said. "I will go and look for Bu-cola. I will not return until I have found her." He put some food into a knapsack and set off.

At mid-day, as he sat eating his bread, he thought, 'The world is a very large place. How am I going to find Bu-cola? I could be walking in the wrong direction.' He was doing up his knapsack when he had an idea. He wondered why he hadn't thought of it before. He stood on the largest rock he could find, and called as loudly as he could,

"Moo if you are alive Bu-cola. Moo now!" And then he put his hand to his ear and he listened.

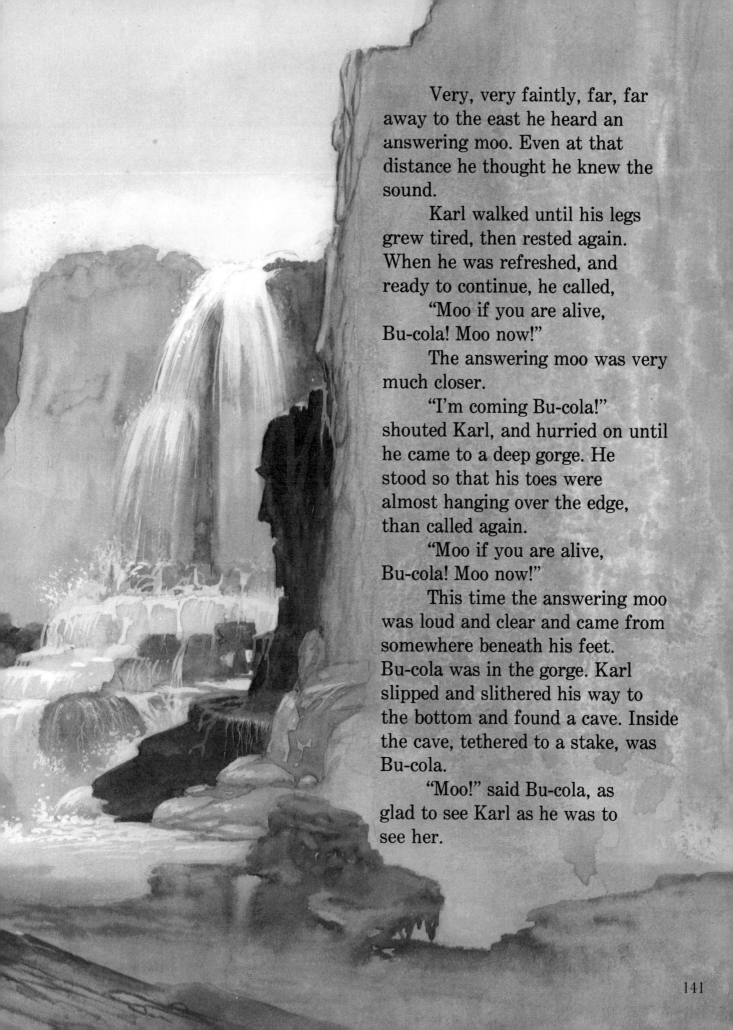

Very, very faintly, far, far away to the east he heard an answering moo. Even at that distance he thought he knew the sound.

Karl walked until his legs grew tired, then rested again. When he was refreshed, and ready to continue, he called,

"Moo if you are alive, Bu-cola! Moo now!"

The answering moo was very much closer.

"I'm coming Bu-cola!" shouted Karl, and hurried on until he came to a deep gorge. He stood so that his toes were almost hanging over the edge, than called again.

"Moo if you are alive, Bu-cola! Moo now!"

This time the answering moo was loud and clear and came from somewhere beneath his feet. Bu-cola was in the gorge. Karl slipped and slithered his way to the bottom and found a cave. Inside the cave, tethered to a stake, was Bu-cola.

"Moo!" said Bu-cola, as glad to see Karl as he was to see her.

Karl untied her and led her up the side of the gorge.

"Now for home," said Karl when they had got to the top and recovered their breath. "Mother will be glad to see you."

They hadn't gone very far when there was the sound of something heavy thudding and thumping behind them. Karl looked back over his shoulder to see what it was, and nearly died of fright. They were being chased by a gigantic troll wife and her troll daughter. They looked very angry. 'That cave must have been theirs,' thought Karl. 'They must think I've stolen Bu-cola from them. They must be coming to get her back!'

"Oh dear, what shall I do?" he cried aloud. "I'm no match for a troll wife."

"Moo!" said Bu-cola. "Pull a hair from my tail and lay it on the ground behind us."

Karl did so at once. This wasn't the time to be asking why, or what for.

"Oh hair of my tail become a deep river that no one can cross!" mooed Bu-cola. Immediately the hair became a raging river, with Karl and Bu-cola on one side of it, and the troll wife and the troll girl on the other.

"Fetch me my great ox!" shouted the troll wife. The ox was a magic one. It drank the river as though it was no more than a puddle. Then, of course, there was nothing to stop the troll wife and the troll girl following Karl and Bu-cola.

"They're getting very close," panted Karl, as the ground shook and trembled beneath their feet.

"Pull a hair from my tail and lay it on the ground behind us!" mooed Bu-cola. "Oh hair of my tail, become a raging fire that no one can cross," she mooed, the instant the hair was on the ground. A wall of leaping flames hid the troll wife and the troll girl from view but it did not hide the sound of the troll wife's voice as she shouted for her ox.

The great ox spat out all the water it had drunk and put out the fire.

143

"Quicker! Quicker!" panted Karl. "The trolls are almost upon us!" The troll shadows had already caught up with them and were looming larger and larger.

"Pull a hair from my tail and lay it on the ground behind us!" mooed Bu-cola urgently. "Oh hair of my tail, become a mountain which no one can cross!" she mooed as it touched the ground. The hair turned into a mountain large enough to stop any troll.

The troll wife's voice rolled round the mountain top like angry thunder as she cried, "Bring me my husband's rock drill!"

"Are we never to escape. . ." gasped Karl. There was the sound of falling rock. Karl snatched a glimpse over his shoulder as he ran. There was a hole breaking through the mountain.

"She's crawling through . . . I can see her head . . ." gasped Karl. "Quicker! Quicker! I can see her shoulders . . ."

But this time the ground did not tremble and shake beneath their feet. This time there were no footsteps thudding behind them. This time there was no dark shadow blotting out the sun. The troll wife was shouting, but she wasn't shouting at them. She was shouting because she was stuck! Her head was sticking out of one side of the mountain. Her feet were sticking out of the other side. She couldn't go forward. She couldn't go backwards. Eventually she turned into mountain stone herself. The troll girl disappeared as though by magic: Karl and Bu-cola were safe.

SEEING IS BELIEVING

Once there was a wizard who sometimes left his secret room and went into the market place. He liked entertaining people with his tricks. They enjoyed it, and so did he.

"Roll up! Roll up!" he cried one day. "Come and see my magic bird!" It wasn't long before a crowd had collected.

"Come on then, show us what it can do!" shouted a boy who was carrying a plank of wood on his shoulder.

"Lend me your plank for a minute or two," said the wizard.

"It won't come to any harm, will it?" asked the boy.

"Of course not. Put it on the ground," said the wizard. He took a cockerel from a sack and put it on the ground beside the plank.

"Watch carefully," he said. He fluttered his fingers over the cockerel and chanted some strange words. To the astonishment of the crowd the cockerel lifted the plank with its beak and began to strut up and down with it.

"How can it do that?" cried the boy whose plank it was. "That's heavy. . .I know. . .I've been carrying it."

Oohs and aahs of astonishment swept through the crowd like a gust of wind.

A girl at the edge of the crowd stood on her tiptoes so that she could see better.

"What's clever about that?" she said. "Any cockerel is strong enough to pick up a straw!" The girl had a four-leaf clover in her hand and could see things exactly as they were. The wizard's magic had fooled everyone else, but it didn't fool her.

Her words were enough to break the spell, and then everyone saw that the cockerel was carrying a straw.

"Cheat! Cheat!" they shouted. The poor wizard, who had only been trying to entertain them, was pelted with cabbages and rotten tomatoes and chased out of town. How everyone laughed at his discomfort. The girl with the four-leaf clover laughed loudest of all.

The months passed, and then one day, there was a village wedding. The villagers were walking in procession across the fields, to the church where the wedding was to be held, when those behind tripped over the heels of those in front. The procession had stopped.

"What is it? What is happening?" asked the people at the back as they jostled to the front to see what was wrong.

They had come to a stream which was far too wide to jump across. There was no bridge over it, and no plank with which to make a bridge.

"We'll have to go back the way we have come, and take the long way round to the church," they cried.

"No! No, we can't do that. I'll be late for my wedding," cried the bride, who was the girl who had found the four-leaf clover.

"Then what shall we do!" they asked her.

In answer the bride kicked off her shoes. She bundled her skirt round her knees and stepped into the stream.

"Brrr . . . it's very cold," she shivered. "Ouch! It's very stony," she winced as she carefully stepped her way across.

"Do not get your wedding dress wet," called the onlookers, those that is, who were not running as fast as their legs would take them the long way round to the church. They began taking off their own shoes, and tucking up their own skirts. The men rolled up their trouser legs. Soon, everyone was wincing and shivering as they followed the bride.

"Where are your eyes that you think that is water?" asked a mocking voice.

All eyes turned towards the bank. They saw the familiar face of the wizard. All eyes looked downwards. Instead of water they were wading through grass and blue flax flowers. They were holding their shoes above their heads. They were all showing their knees. The wizard was having the last laugh, and now it was they who had the red faces. How foolish they looked and how foolish they felt.

THE DRUMMER

One evening a drummer boy was walking beside the lake when he saw three pieces of fine white linen. He took one of the pieces home with him and laid it across the foot of his bed.

That night, just as he was going to sleep, a voice said, "Drummer, give me my shift." He rubbed his eyes sleepily and saw a girl standing at the foot of his bod.

"I will, if you tell me who you are" he said.

"I am the daughter of a king. I have fallen under the spell of a witch. She lets me bathe once a day in the lake with my sisters. My sisters have gone but I cannot return until I have my shift." She picked up the piece of white linen.

"Wait!" cried the Drummer. "Before you go, tell me how I can help you."

"You can free me from the witch if you can reach the top of the glass mountain, but that is impossible. Even if you find it the sides are too steep to climb."

"Where is the glass mountain?" asked the Drummer.

"All I can tell you is that the road you must take goes through the forest where the giants live," said the girl, and then she went.

As soon as it was light, the Drummer took the road leading through the forest. He beat loudly
on his drum which roused a giant who had been lying asleep in the grass.

"What are you drumming for, you impudent boy?" demanded the giant, who didn't like being woken so rudely.

"To show the way to the thousands who follow me."

"What do they want in the forest?" asked the giant.

"To kill you, and all like you," said the Drummer.

"Don't be foolish," laughed the giant. "We giants will trample you like ants."

"We will creep on you like ants when you are asleep and hit you with steel hammers," said the Drummer.

The giant didn't like the sound of that at all. "Stop drumming," he said, "and I'll do anything you ask."

"Carry me to the glass mountain," said the Drummer.

"I can only take you part of the way," said the giant. "My two brothers will take you the rest."

151

The giant's second brother carried the Drummer to the foot of the glass mountain. It was three times as high as an ordinary mountain and quite impossible to climb.

"If only I was a bird," sighed the Drummer. He was sitting on a grassy hillock trying to work out what to do when he saw two men quarrelling over a saddle.

"You are stupid to quarrel over a saddle when you have no horse to put it on," he said.

"Not as stupid as you think," said the men. "Sit on this saddle and wish, and you can go wherever you want to go."

"Can you indeed!" said the Drummer. "Then let me settle your quarrel for you." He went a short distance and put a stick in the ground. When he returned he said, "Whoever reaches the stick first wins the saddle."

As soon as the men began to run the Drummer sat on the saddle and made a wish to himself.

Suddenly he was at the top of the glass mountain where there was a little house, a fishpond and a pine forest. He knocked at the door of the house. An old witch who opened it said she would give him food and a bed for the night if he would perform three tasks for her.

The Drummer's first task was to empty the pond with a thimble, and sort the fishes. He worked hard, and long, but the water in the pond never seemed to get less. Towards evening a girl came from the house and spoke to him.

"You look tired," she said. "Lay your head in my lap and sleep. When you wake your task will be done."

When the Drummer was asleep the girl twisted the ring on her finger and made a wish. The water rose from the pond in a fine mist and floated away. The fish jumped about and sorted themselves.

When the Drummer woke, the girl said, "When the old witch asks why one fish is lying by itself, throw it at her and say, 'That one is for you, old witch'."

The Drummer did exactly as the girl told him. The witch said nothing, but she looked at him very strangely.

The Drummer's second task was to cut down all the trees in the forest and split them into logs. An impossible task, even with a sharp axe, and the axe the witch had given him was blunt.

At midday the girl came from the house, and said, "You look very tired. Lay your head in my lap and sleep."

When the Drummer woke he found the second task completed.

"When the old witch asks why one log lies apart from the others," said the girl, "give her a blow with it and say, 'That is for you old witch!'"

The Drummer did exactly as he was told. The witch looked at him very strangely, but she said nothing. The third task she set him was to pile all the logs together and burn them in one huge fire. The girl came from the house and once more told him to sleep. When he woke the flames were leaping and the logs were burning fiercely.

"You must do whatever the witch tells you to do without fear," said the girl before she went back into the house.

The witch came and watched the flames leaping and curling.

"Look," she said. "There is a log right in the middle of the fire which is not burning. Bring it to me."

The Drummer jumped, without fear, into the heart of the fire and brought out the log. As the log touched the ground it turned into the girl who had been helping him. Then he saw that she was the Princess he had come to rescue.

"You shall not have her!" screeched the witch, and leapt forward to push her into the flames, but the Drummer was quicker than the witch. It was the witch who fell into the flames, not the Princess. That was the end of the witch!

155

The Drummer and the Princess filled their pockets with treasure from the witch's house and went home.

"Do not kiss your parents on the right cheek when you greet them," said the Princess. "If you do, you will forget me."

In the excitement at being home the Drummer kissed his parents on both cheeks, and all memory of the Princess faded from his mind.

The Princess did not forget the Drummer. When she heard a marriage had been arranged for him she wished for a dress as golden as the sun. She took it to the palace which the Drummer had built with his share of the witch's treasure.

"What a beautiful dress," sighed the girl who was to be the Drummer's bride. "Oh, I do wish it was mine."

"I will give it to you if you will let me sit outside the Drummer's room tonight," said the Princess.

The girl wanted the dress so much she agreed, but before the Drummer went to bed that night, she gave him a sleeping potion.

During the night the Princess opened the door to the Drummer's room and called softly,

"Dear Drummer, are you awake?"

The Drummer was sleeping so soundly he did not hear her and she went sadly away.

The next day she wished for a dress as silvery as the moon, and went to the palace. The bride-to-be agreed to let the Princess spend another night outside the Drummer's room in exchange for the dress, but she made sure he drank another sleeping potion before he went to bed. Once again he slept soundly and did not hear when the Princess called.

On the third day the Princess wished for a dress that glistened like the stars. The same thing happened, but that night the Drummer did not drink the sleeping potion. When the Princess called softly, "Dear Drummer, are you awake?" he heard her. The sound of her voice was enough to restore his memory.

"You are my true bride," he said.

So, there was a change in the wedding plans. The Drummer married the Princess. As for the girl who was to have been his bride, she had the three most beautiful dresses in the world, so they all lived happily ever after.